Royal House of Leone

The PRINCESS'S
SCANDALOUS
AFFAIR

by Jennifer Lewis

1

"Now that your brother has vanquished me, will you join me for a drink?"

Beatriz Leone turned to see the son of an ancient family with an equally ancient grudge against hers. Lorenzo Aldobrando had been pointed out to her earlier at this festival of conspicuous consumption that was her twin brother's coronation.

She looked at her mom, part of the conversation circle she'd been stuck in for twenty minutes, in a silent plea for help. "Of course, darling, go on."

Not at all the kind of help she'd wanted. Could she really make a fuss here in front of everyone? Her assailant had been sporting enough to joust her brother on horseback in a traditional rite. Everyone could see he'd allowed himself to be beaten. Which was lucky since her brother wasn't much of a rider, let alone jouster.

"Sure," she said bravely. He extended his arm. She hesitated for a moment, then reluctantly slipped hers inside it. "Lead the way."

Well, this was awkward. She could feel the thick muscles of his arm through his suit. He was far too handsome for his own good and knew it. She hated him already.

Even in her sleek black gown Beatriz felt like the frumpiest person in existence. Why would he want to spend time with her?

"Do you remember beating me at tennis when we were both twelve?" he asked after they were away from the group.

"No." She didn't even remember meeting him before, though she certainly knew of him. "Do you still have hard feelings?"

"I think I'm over it, but I'm always up for a rematch." His eyes twinkled with amusement. They were a cool shade of gray, and other girls probably lost control of themselves staring into them. Maybe Lorenzo thought she'd be the same. He was wrong.

"I don't really play tennis anymore." She tried to sound bored. Which wasn't hard.

"What do you do?" He retrieved two full glasses from one of the champagne tables and handed her one.

What do I do? The eternal question. "I'm the quiet one. Hadn't you heard?"

"Rigo did tell me you still live at home with your mother."

"That makes it sound like I live in her basement. It's a palace with forty-two bedrooms." What else had her brother told him? And why?

He chuckled. "You never moved out?"

"No." She'd always thought she would…one day. But she wasn't academic enough to go to a top university like all her genius brothers and sisters. And her father had almost ruptured a gut laughing when she said she wanted to study fashion. "I like it here. And my mother needs me."

"I was so sorry to hear of the loss of your father and grandmother." His eyes filled with what looked charmingly like genuine sorrow. So he was a good actor. Did he know that he'd been on their list of suspects? If she discovered that he was the man who'd murdered her beloved father, she'd kill him herself.

"It was a horrible shock. Mom is still really cut up by it. If I was thinking of moving away, I couldn't do it now. I'm the only one left."

"I think it's very kind of you to stay here and support her."

She peered at him sideways over her champagne glass. Was he poking fun at her?

"Someone's got to. What do you do?" Anything to get the conversation off herself. After a couple more minutes of this, she could make an excuse and slip away.

"I suppose I'm like you. I got suckered into the family business." His eyes sparkled again. Was she supposed to be charmed by this? "My father inherited a lot of properties from his father, and I've been managing them."

"I heard you tried to obtain a lease to the property on Sarn lake." She watched closely for his reaction. Did he think she'd have no clue about family business?

He lifted a brow. "Yes, I asked Darias twice with no success."

She raised herself up to her full height. Which was

still several inches shorter than him even in these uncomfortable heels. "That's because the house is mine now. My grandmother left it to me."

His eyes showed a hint of surprise. Which was probably fake. The lake house must be the reason he'd approached her. It still sat empty, except of cobwebs, and—as the recent scene of two grisly murders—no doubt looked like a potential bargain. "Really?"

"Really." She wished she could just put down her glass and leave. Property transfers were a matter of public record, which he'd know since he was in the business. "If you're still hoping to lease it, I'm afraid it won't be available. I have plans for it."

"That's great news. It's such a fine old house in a magical setting. It's a shame for it to be sitting neglected."

She hadn't given any serious thought to the property, but she wasn't going to let this character think it might be available. "My plans aren't final yet. I might turn it into a hotel."

The last part was a bold-faced lie. She just wanted to see his reaction.

"Isn't it rather remote for that?"

"That would be part of the appeal." His family owned the land on the other side of the lake—in Italy. "What were you planning to do with it?"

"I hadn't formed any concrete plans." He smiled and sipped his champagne. "Which is lucky since they would have come to nothing."

She didn't believe him. Her family speculated that he had plans to turn the remote lake into a tourist destination to rival Lake Como, which would be more profitable if he owned all the land around it. And she didn't think he'd give up so easily, either. "Oh, look, there's Vittorio! I haven't seen him in ages! Do excuse me." She took off across the room, heading into a knot of people. When she reached one of her dad's old hunting buddies, she accosted him like a long-lost lover.

It was a huge relief to get away from Lorenzo. His flashy good looks annoyed her and his boundless confidence unsettled her. Probably due to her own low self-esteem.

She babbled on about her dad with Vittorio, who seemed as devastated as her by his loss, though their conversation focused on the growing population of deer in the hills this winter. Possibly due to her dad not being out hunting them every day.

"May I have this dance?" A low voice in her ear made her spin around. Lorenzo again! He had nerve to butt in when she'd just managed to escape him.

"Oh, do go on, my dear. Your papa wouldn't want you standing around jawing with an old codger like me when a handsome young swain wants to take you on the floor." Vittorio obviously didn't recognize Lorenzo as one of their ancient enemies, the Aldobrandos. Which wasn't surprising as Lorenzo didn't live in Altaleone and rarely came here.

Once again she found herself being swept away by him. This time he held her hand firmly—which she hated as it heated her palm and sent an odd sensation up her arm. He guided her—or dragged her—to the dance floor, while the band played a boppy dance number. She shot him a look of mild exasperation to let him know she wasn't fooled even for a second into thinking that he might be interested in her.

There were far more beautiful women here

tonight. Some were even princesses like her. "Nice try, running away from me." He leaned in and his warm breath rushed against her skin. "When we'd barely even exchanged hellos."

"What do you want with me?" He'd been bold, so she could be, too.

He laughed. "What a question! I'm intrigued by you, Beatriz." The way he said her name, slow and soft, should have sounded like an insult but instead it felt like a caress.

Disturbing.

"Why?" It was a fair question. Of course he didn't have personal experience with how dull she was, but surely her reputation preceded her.

"You're an enigma. A beautiful woman with great assets and opportunities at her disposal, living a life of quiet retreat."

"What's wrong with that? You make me sound like a medieval nun, but I'm quite busy. Royals don't sit around all day doing needlepoint, as I'm sure you're aware. My mother and I opened a new supermarket on the road to Laverno last week, and this week there's the primary school awards ceremony."

He had the gall to look amused, as if these weren't real work. Which they weren't. Doing one thing a week hardly constituted a job. "And I have a horse who needs to be ridden."

"I didn't accuse you of being lazy." He had the decency to look contrite. "Just that you don't seem to have the grand ambition of other members of your family."

"Of my siblings, you mean. My parents both enjoy a quiet home life." Ouch. She'd just spoken of her dad as if he were still alive. "My dad and I used to ride together every day. I miss him so much I can barely stand it." She let her pain show in her voice. She wasn't under any obligation to make Lorenzo Aldobrando feel comfortable.

They were barely dancing, just swaying slightly in time to the music. A slow song started, and to her alarm he pulled her into his arms. "I can't imagine your pain. He was so young and full of life."

"Why would anyone want to kill him?" She asked herself the question several times a day, and it came out on a sob. "He wasn't even king. He never hurt anyone."

Lorenzo stroked her back. "Your family still has no idea why?"

"No." She looked up at him, suddenly suspicious. Was he probing to see what they suspected? If he was guilty he could, then relax in the knowledge that they were still clueless. "Do you have any insight?"

He drew in a breath and frowned. "I wish I did. I've spent very little time in Altaleone."

"But you're friends with Rigo?"

"We met at a sailing course near Rome when we were teens. We've stayed in touch. I meet him for dinner when I'm in New York."

Interesting. Her brother Rigo was a hard man to like and an excellent—if harsh—judge of character. As a lawyer he was used to picking people's arguments apart and could see right through even the most carefully constructed facade.

"We wish Rigo would spend more time here. Perhaps he'd have the insight we need to figure out who's behind this."

"I'd like that, too. I plan to spend more time in the area." He flashed those dangerous slate-gray eyes again. To her horror a responding flare happened somewhere deep inside her. Damn him! How could he have this effect on her? He was just another self-assured asshat who expected the world to bow to his will. "And I'd very much like to spend more time with you."

Here's where she should tell him how terribly busy she was. Except they'd already established that wasn't the case. "Oh." She tried to be noncommittal—or was it rude?

His arms held her close and her body started to react in a disturbing way. Heat gathered low in her belly, and her traitorous nipples tightened beneath the demure dark silk of her dress.

The sooner she could get away, the better. "I have to go."

She pulled from his grasp and started to walk toward the nearest door. It led into a hallway and—unfortunately—he followed her out.

"What day is good for you to go out to lunch this week?"

"We have a lot of guests right now because of my brother's coronation. I really can't get away." She glanced to the left and right. The left was empty and led back toward the kitchens. Surely he wouldn't follow her there?

Unfortunately, he did. He kept close enough to speak at an almost whisper.

"Does it bother you that your brother is now king, even though you're twins?"

She shivered slightly. Of course it bothered her. She shrugged and tried to keep her breathing steady. "That's just the way it is. I've known since I was tiny that the male heir inherits, regardless of who was born first."

He took hold of her wrist, stopping her forward motion. "You were born first?"

"By fifteen minutes, yes. But who cares about that?" She tried to get her hand back but not hard enough to create a scene.

He held firm. "If it were me, I might be a little bitter." Those penetrating eyes seemed to see right into her soul.

Which was impossible, thank goodness. Sometimes she wasn't sure she even had a soul. "Well, I'm not. We're a family, and I don't think Darias was all that excited about being king anyway."

"I heard he's a well-known artist."

"And he had a great life in New York City so maybe he'd have preferred for me to take the crown. But we don't get to pick and choose. Being born royal you learn to accept that you have responsibilities to your family and to your country."

He looked at her steadily, still holding her hand, which grew hot inside his. Her words hung in the air between them, suddenly sounding pompous and overblown.

"You're a credit to your family." He spoke softly, with every appearance of being sincere. "And I find you strikingly beautiful."

Strikingly beautiful? What was that supposed to mean? She'd been told she was horse-faced and also that she had the family nose. She was pretty sure neither was meant as a compliment.

Beatriz wondered how many times he'd used that line. And why was he still staring at her like this? His gaze roamed over her face, heating the skin over her cheekbones, her chin, making her mouth twitch.

She attempted to gather the strength to pull her hand back but something about the way he stared at her held her frozen, like a rabbit in the sights of a predator who hopes that by not moving it will be rendered invisible.

Lorenzo raised her hand to his mouth and pressed his lips to it. Not to the back or to her fingers, like they did in the movies, but he gently turned it over and touched his mouth to her palm. The sensations that rushed through her made her blink.

It took a moment before she could summon the wherewithal to tug her hand back, and to her surprise he let it go. A look of regret lingered in his gaze. "You are a very unique woman, Princess Beatriz."

"Not really," she protested, cursing herself for being lame. Should she start running toward the kitchens from here? Or should she dash back to the party? "I really have to go."

"I understand." His arms hung at his sides. He wore elegant black tie as easily as if it were athletic wear. "And I look forward to speaking with you again under less formal circumstances."

The kitchen it was. She pivoted and headed down the darkening corridor, toward the servants' quarters. She didn't dare risk a glance back because she had a horrible feeling that he'd be standing there staring after her.

She resolved, then and there, to make sure she was never in the same room with Lorenzo Aldobrando again in this lifetime.

2

Lorenzo sat down in the ski lift next to his friend and sometime business partner, Rafi Santos. They'd just skied down a double black diamond run and were headed to the top of one called the Widowmaker. "It's hard to find a challenge these days. We've skied every run on both sides of the Alps, and we both know we have the best skiing in the world right here."

"We may have to look into a new area for a challenge." Rafi pulled his gloves on as the lift rose high up over the steep mountainside, with its white ribbons of ski runs diving and dodging through the pine forest below. "Still no dice on the Lake Sarn project? I flew over it again last week when I took my new plane up for a spin. Gorgeous lake and great access from north and south, and you already own the land on the far side. Could be the next Lake Como. And that looks like a good ski mountain to the north of the lake. Cut some runs and build a lift and you'll be making money all year 'round."

"I had two firm nos from Darias—or his office— last summer, but then I learned the oldest daughter inherited it."

"The hot redhead? I heard she's a scientist working in Paris these days. Something to do with genetics."

"Not her. That's Callista. Beatriz is the eldest."

"Beatriz?" Rafi peered at the scenery. "I don't remember that one."

"She's a brunette. Quiet. Still lives at home."

"Sounds dull." He glanced up. "Shame or you could marry into the property."

His friend laughed, and Lorenzo laughed with him. "I don't think I need to take it that far."

"You'll just seduce her into leasing it to you?"

It was annoying that his friend could see right through him. "I'd settle for a lease but I'd prefer to buy it. No one in the family has lived in it for decades. She claims she has plans to turn it into a hotel, but there's been no progress there since the summer. I've been keeping an eye on it, and not a single tree has been trimmed. It would need a new road bulldozed through the mountains for decent access on the Altaleone side of the lake."

"When you rule your own country a little bulldozing is not a big problem." Rafi winked.

They were drawing near the peak, so Lorenzo pulled his skiing goggles down over his eyes. "I don't believe she intends to do anything with it. She was just brushing me off like a fly."

"You?" Rafi lifted a brow. "I don't imagine you'd take that lying down."

"I don't intend to." He stared ahead at the horizon, where jagged white peaks poked up into the harsh blue sky. "I plan to warm her up to me, no matter how many layers of ice I have to chisel through."

"Ha! I remember that time you lost a crampon down the gorge near Mt. Althorn. She has no idea how adept you are on sheer, slick ice."

"Right? I'll make it worth her while. I already have a vision for the buildings. The old house was built with stone from a quarry right near the site. We could mine it ourselves. It's likely cheaper than bringing stone in down these mountain roads."

"I can't imagine the Leone family would be too thrilled with you mining their precious countryside."

"They won't have a say if I own it. Besides, I can dig the quarry on the land we already own, so it's not even in Altaleone but in Italy."

"Shame you only own a sliver of frontage on the lake."

"Damn shame. Blame my ancestor Wilfredo Aldobrando and his gambling addiction for that. We probably would have been able to buy and sell Altaleone by now if it wasn't for him decimating the family estates."

Rafi cracked up. "You aristos sure hold a grudge! When was that, five hundred years ago?"

"More like eight hundred." Lorenzo sighed. "But it is a beautiful piece of land."

"But is the girl beautiful?"

They'd reached the top of the lift, and Lorenzo put a pole in each hand ready to jump off onto an almost sheer drop. He could see the ice gleaming from here, and it sent a spike of adrenaline through him. "Yes. She is."

"Beatriz, darling, could you do me a favor and find Papa's old business cards?" Beatriz heard her mom call her from outside the library. "I can't remember what font he used. I want to get some made for Darias."

"No problem, Mama." She put her book back on the shelf. She had no idea what her mom would say if she'd replied that sorry, she was busy. But, since that never happened, it was hardly a worry.

She walked down the few doors to her father's old study. The soft, sweet smell of his pipe tobacco lingered in the carpet and curtains and hit her like a punch to the gut. She couldn't believe she'd never see him again. His death had been so sudden and unexpected that it still felt like a bad dream.

She pulled open the top drawer of his desk, feeling like an intruder. He'd never have let her do this if he were alive. His study was his private realm where even the most trusted staff had to tread lightly and ask permission to touch anything. The drawer was cluttered and disorganized, perhaps from being gone through by Gibran's security forces looking for any clues as to who might have killed him.

She knew they'd found something odd. There was a lot of hushed whispering, but no one had told her about it and her mom claimed to be in the dark too. She closed the drawer, half afraid to even look through the mysterious crumpled papers, and opened a silver box on top of the desk. Cigars. Her phone rang, and she glanced at it. Unknown number.

She didn't usually answer calls from mystery numbers. It was family policy. Too many journalists out there looking for a story by asking leading questions. But after the mad rush of Christmas and an onslaught of houseguests, the house was empty and she felt bored and reckless. "Hello?"

"Beatriz, it's Lorenzo." His deep voice shot through her like a bullet.

She stood straight up. "What do you want?" The

suspicion in her voice embarrassed her. She'd wondered if he would call—for a week, maybe a full month. As the weeks and months dragged on she'd grown bitter that he hadn't ever bothered.

Now all of a sudden he was calling her out of nowhere?

"I was hoping things have settled down enough at the palace for you to have lunch with me."

"Settled down? You mean since the coronation?" She laughed. "It's been more than six months."

"I know you were busy."

Everyone knows I'm never busy. "You know how it is." Her two closest friends had both moved away from Altaleone in the last year. One to marry a banker in Zurich and the other for a job as a translator at the United Nations. Her mom and Emma, Darias's new wife, were the only people she'd even been out for lunch with in ages.

"Is there a day this week that would work? I'm in Altaleone right now."

Was he at the hotel in the village? She hated the idea of running into him. "Oh." And there was absolutely no way she'd consider having lunch with him after he'd flirted with her shamelessly, then blown her off for six solid months. "Actually I have a lot going on this week." She was going to reorganize her underwear drawer, for one thing. And she had these business cards to find...

She spotted the cards in a tortoiseshell holder half hidden behind a big paperweight.

"I could come by and pick you up today."

"Today?" It was almost lunchtime right now. "I don't think that would be a good idea."

"Lunch or me picking you up? I know our families

15

are ancient enemies, but I think we could put all that behind us."

"I wasn't even thinking—"

"Beatriz!" Her mom's voice jerked her attention to the open doorway. "Did you find them yet? I'm putting together a list of items for the engraver."

She sighed. Her life really was one boring chore after another. At least if she had lunch with this entitled jerk it would be a break from the monotony. "I'll meet you in the village at twelve-thirty," she said with sudden resolve. "Do you know where Rialto, the stationary store, is?"

"Of course. I'll see you there." She could already hear the satisfaction in his voice. Perhaps he thought she'd be eating out of his hand by twelve forty-five. At least no one from the palace would see her on this fool's errand, and the store was down a quiet side street, away from prying eyes.

She picked up a business card and wiped off a thin layer of dust that had already formed on it. Then she carried it out into the hallway, where her mom was rushing around in the middle of something. "Mom, I found it. It's too old-fashioned for Darias, though." She showed her the old-fashioned script. Her dad was marvelously Old World. She used to tease him that he was born in the wrong century and he wholeheartedly agreed. "I'm sure Darias would prefer something clean and modern."

"I suppose you're right, darling. Perhaps you could nip over to the castle and ask him."

I'm sorry, I'm far too busy. I'm having lunch with Lorenzo Aldobrando. She couldn't even begin to imagine what kind of a reaction that announcement would get. "Sure, I'll do it today." She took the card and put it in her pocket. She could kill two birds with one stone and visit Darias after her lunch date in town.

Wait. It wasn't a date. It was simply a lunch. Lorenzo would probably ask her all kinds of questions about the Sarn Lake property—how her hotel was coming along and other nonsense—then try to lease it or buy it. She wasn't deluded enough to think for even one minute that he was interested in her.

Beatriz decided to walk into the village so no one would notice her car parked somewhere for a long period of time. She took her dad's old business card and walked to the castle first. It was right in the town center, up on a hill, and she greeted the guards as she entered. Her brother was in a meeting with one of the business managers but came out as soon as she was announced.

"Beatriz, hey, what's up?" Still not exactly king material. But she couldn't fault Darias for that. He wasn't supposed to be king for many decades. "If you're looking for Emma, she went to drop some books off at the hospital library. She should be back soon."

"I can't come here just to see you?" Even though her brother was home now, and not in New York, they might as well still have the Atlantic between them. Then he was too busy being a famous artist; now he was preoccupied with being king. "Actually don't worry, I'm here on family business, as usual." She pulled out the card. "I know you've been up all night worrying about what your business cards should look like, so Mom wanted you to take a look at Dad's."

Darias explained that no one used cards anymore since they could just text each other their information, and she told him to pick a font anyway to make their mom happy. The entire exchange took less than five minutes, then she was on her way again.

After she left the castle she took a slight detour to kill a few minutes and in case anyone was watching, then turned down the side street where she'd arranged to meet Lorenzo.

She spotted him as he climbed out of his midnight blue Audi. His dark hair looked windswept, as if he'd driven straight from the ski slopes. She cursed the way her heart thumped when he saw her and waved.

She waved back, then regretted it. She needed to play it cool. She wasn't going to give him the idea that he could wrap her around his little finger and then take advantage of her.

"Hi, Beatriz. I'm so glad you could make it. I made reservations at Andante."

"That sounds fine." At least Andante was very private. There were only a handful of tables so hardly anyone would see her there with him.

They walked together down the street, past the town's quaint houses. "I'm sorry it took me so long to call." He looked genuinely contrite. "To be honest I could tell you were trying to get away from me. I decided to give you time to wait until you forgot about me so we could start over."

His quirky smile made her laugh. "You're quite perceptive. I was overwhelmed by the crowds at the coronation and still very much on the ropes after my father's death. I just wanted to be alone with my grief."

Lorenzo had been the only one to observe that

being the older twin of the man being crowned king must have hurt too. It had taken her a while to put that behind her.

"It seems like I picked the right time."

"We'll see." She lifted a brow.

His smile told her that he didn't mind her arch candor. Maybe he liked it. Like herself he was rich and entitled and probably sick of people fawning all over him.

He stood aside so she could enter the restaurant, and the maître d' greeted her with perfect formal politeness and her correct title and showed them to a table way in the back, with high-backed benches. It was unlikely anyone could see them or overhear their conversation here. She wondered if he'd requested that when he made the reservation.

She sat down on plush cushions and sipped her water. If anything, Lorenzo was even better-looking than she remembered. His eyes were a lighter gray than she recalled—almost blue.

He ordered champagne for the table without asking whether she wanted any. Things took another turn for the worse when he talked about the weather and skiing conditions, and Beatriz had to admit that she hadn't been skiing once all winter. It was yet another activity she had shared with her dad. A pang of sorrow was about to turn into a violent urge to be alone when Lorenzo changed the subject.

"I just got back from Milan. My sister Steffi bought a boutique in Zurich and needed to visit the designers to choose some stock. She talked me into accompanying her."

Beatriz eyes widened. "Which designers?"

"We visited Prada, Dolce & Gabbana, Armani…all

the usual suspects, and some young designers just out of fashion school. I think she's secretly hoping to discover the next big name."

"How exciting. I love Giovanna Batti's new collection with rose-shaped buckles."

His eyes widened. "She bought several pieces from that one. You follow fashion?"

"Yes, I've always been interested in it. I mostly follow it in magazines, but every now and then I go to Milan to see the shows."

She hadn't done that in ages. Not since her sister Mari had left for college. They used to go together.

"I'm surprised. You don't seem like someone who'd follow trends." He had the decency not to glance at her rather frumpy outfit. Today she wore a black cashmere sweater and black pants. "Your style is more classic."

She laughed. "Occupational hazard."

"Not really. Other European royals sometimes seize on the latest trends. Maybe you should give your passions free rein and wear something daring and different."

She recoiled at the idea of giving her passions free rein. Right now she was having enough trouble staying calm. Her fingers accidentally brushed Lorenzo's as he handed her a glass of champagne, and the resulting frisson of sensation almost made her jump.

She sipped her champagne, trying to cover her confusion. "I'm actually not that interested in wearing the latest styles." Wow, that made her sound really dull. Could she try to be slightly less of a bore? "I'm more intrigued by the design aspect. I like to draw a collection and then stack it up against what actually comes out that season."

"What?" Lorenzo looked and sounded so stunned that she instantly regretted her confession. "You're a closet designer? I must see your designs."

"Oh, goodness, no. They're just a hobby. Something to keep me busy in between handing out trophies at school events."

"I'm absolutely riveted." He stared at her, disbelief in his eyes, champagne glass in midair. "But I shouldn't be so surprised. I had a feeling there was something different about you. Do you ever get your designs made into a wearable sample?"

"Oh, no. That would be silly when there are already so many great designers. Mine are just for my own entertainment."

"But wouldn't you love to see your creation on someone?"

She shrugged, wishing she could think of a way to change the subject. "I suppose, but who'd want to wear them?"

He laughed. "You're a princess. Half of Europe would want to wear them." He sipped his champagne. "I'm beginning to wonder if your naiveté is an act. I don't think anyone could actually be as unselfconscious as you seem to be.

"Unfortunately I'm just as unexciting as I seem." She sipped her champagne again, then decided she'd better carefully monitor her intake. It wouldn't be a good idea to get tipsy around this guy. "Sorry to disappoint."

He leaned back in his chair and narrowed his eyes. A sly smile crept across his lips. "I have a strange feeling that you're a fantastic butterfly—with colorful, patterned wings like no one has ever seen before—

but you're stuck deep in your royal chrysalis and can't figure out how to get out.".

3

Beatriz tried to think of a witty comeback but failed. Another sign that she wasn't the woman he anticipated. Though sometimes she did wonder if being royal had limited her options rather than expanded them. What would she be doing now if she'd been able to try and fail and find her way in the world like a regular person?

The waiter rattled off that day's specials, and she chose a roasted pork loin with a beetroot compote. Lorenzo selected veal medallions and ordered a truffle ravioli appetizer for them to share. She could resent him ordering for her. However, since it sounded so good she didn't mind.

"Did you go to fashion college?" he asked, after the waiter had left. "Milan has one of the best in the world, but I know most of your siblings went to school in the U.S."

"No." She tried to smile. "I thought about it but never got around to it." She didn't want to blame her father aloud. He didn't want to see her fail. Or didn't want to lose his hunting buddy. She could forgive him for both. "I just do my designs for fun."

"I'd really like to see them. Do you have any on your phone?"

She blinked. Why was he so interested? No one ever wanted to see her drawings. Even her mom just smiled at them and said, "That's nice, dear."

"I have a couple, I guess. I sometimes send them to my sister Mari. She likes fashion too." She pulled out her phone, heart thumping. She wasn't sure if it was anxiety over how he'd react to her designs or if she was unsettled by that intense stare of his.

She flipped through her photos—which were a showcase of how boring her life had become. Pictures of Christmas decorations from last Christmas, fabric ideas for new curtains for Emma and Darias's bedroom. A bird she'd seen outside in the snow.

At last she found a sketch she'd done for an evening dress. She clicked on it and kept hold of the phone so he couldn't start scrolling around. "This dress was inspired by my new sister-in-law, Emma. She makes everything look fabulous, but I thought this would drape over her well." The dress was a bias-cut design with an asymmetrical hem and neckline, and she'd added a necklace to balance the asymmetry. "It's supposed to be silver. Or gold. I couldn't decide. Maybe something in the middle."

Ugh. She regretted rambling on. He didn't care what color it was supposed to be. He must be cringing inwardly for her and thinking about how to change the subject.

The waiter arrived far too fast with the ravioli and sprinkled them with fresh pepper. Lorenzo still hadn't looked up from her phone. Her hand was starting to shake from holding it. Exasperated and embarrassed, she pulled it back. So what if he didn't want to say anything.

"It would look amazing on Emma. You should

make it for her as a surprise." His eyes shone with unexpected warmth.

"Do you really think so?" She put her phone away. "She loves neutral colors, but I thought a little flash would look so gorgeous on her."

"And I think it's sweet that you were thinking of your sister-in-law. I heard the story of how your brother basically bought her company for a year. A lot of sisters wouldn't have been so understanding."

Beatriz stuck a fork into one of the plump ravioli. "She had her reasons. Her brother is a drug addict, and she was trying to help him. Don't think I didn't give her a hard time about it." She took a bite. The flavor was so exquisite it almost stole her breath—which was a nice distraction from Lorenzo, who no doubt thought he was the most delicious thing at the table. "Emma's lovely, and so sweet with Mama."

"Does she like the design?"

"I haven't showed it to her. I don't think she's too interested in fashion. I suspect that left to her own devices she'd wear jeans and sneakers every day. You know how Americans are."

Lorenzo laughed. "You're so funny! I can't believe you didn't even show her. Has she seen any of your designs?"

Beatriz racked her mind for a second. "No. I just do them for myself. There's no need to bore anyone else with them."

Lorenzo stared at her, his gaze hardening. "I'm growing quite exasperated with you, Beatriz. You have a ferocious talent, and you're not even showing your ideas to anyone."

"My sister Mari liked it."

Lorenzo picked up a ravioli and ate it whole. He

stared at her the whole time he was chewing. She tried to ignore him by cutting up the rest of her ravioli and eating it slowly, but she was sure that her face must be reddening. His scrutiny was unnerving.

When he'd finally finished his mouthful and taken a swig of champagne, he leaned back in his chair. "I'd like to commission that dress."

"What?" He startled her so much she almost spilled her champagne, which she was drinking way too fast. "Who for?"

"For you." His steady gray gaze bored into her.

"Me? It wouldn't suit me at all. It needs someone more…statuesque. I'm too short."

"You're not short at all. What are you, five-seven?"

"Five-six. And I couldn't carry it off. Besides, the dressmaker we normally use wouldn't know what to do with it, even if I could find the right fabric."

Lorenzo smiled. "No, the guy who shortens the hems of your dresses couldn't pull this off. But my sister Steffi will know of someone. Like I said, we just toured several Milan ateliers. I'll call her right now."

Before she could protest he'd pulled out his phone and was talking rapidly in Italian to his sister Steffi, whom she dimly remembered doing a French immersion course in the Loire Valley with one summer.

He hung up the phone with a satisfied smile. "She says Signora Pazzi is the best—and fast. We must plan a trip to Milan."

"What? That's hours away."

"Less than two. And it's a scenic drive."

"I'm not sure I can get away." This was going way too far, too fast. She couldn't shake the feeling that somehow she was the butt of a joke.

"How's tomorrow? I don't have anything all day. We could leave after breakfast and be back by late afternoon."

She blinked. She didn't actually have any plans for tomorrow. Or the rest of the week, truth be told. And she'd love to see the inside of a real Milan atelier. Her family had everything made locally so she'd never had the excuse—except during fashion week when everything was about display, not the far more interesting behind-the-scenes stuff.

"I suppose I could. If you're sure we'll be back before dark." She had no intention of telling anyone where she was going. They'd freak if they knew she was with Lorenzo Aldobrando. He wasn't exactly a suspect in the murders, but her brother Darias didn't seem to trust him, either.

"On my honor." He placed a hand on his heart. Strangely, she believed that Lorenzo was a man of honor. Perhaps just because she'd seen him dressed in armor atop a magnificent horse and jousting during the coronation ceremonies. The sight was undeniably impressive—even more so when you knew how handsome the knight was beneath his armor. "We'll meet here in town and go in my car. We can meet in the same place, on Letissa Street."

She bit her lip. This was a chance to see one of her own designs come to life. "Okay. I still think you're crazy, but I'll do it."

"Excellent." Their main courses had arrived, and Lorenzo attacked his food with gusto. "You won't regret it. And I suspect it will be the start of a new chapter in your life."

Beatriz inhaled slowly. *Beatriz Leone, designer.* It had a nice ring to it. Then she remembered her dad's laughter. *Really, Bea? What would people say?* He had no respect for fashion as an art and thought it was a silly waste of time.

But he was gone now and wouldn't even know. And if it didn't work out—if the dress looked terrible, or the seamstress laughed at her design and said it was impossible, or Lorenzo turned out to be poking fun at her—no one would know. It was her secret. Everyone around here had so many damn secrets, maybe it was finally her turn.

She ate a forkful of pork. It was tender and delicious, as you'd expect at such a fine old restaurant. She was glad that being royal and privileged hadn't spoiled her for enjoyment of the hard work and expertise of others. And, just for now, she was going to give him the benefit of the doubt. "Thank you, Lorenzo. I'm looking forward to it."

The next morning, Lorenzo parked outside the stationer's shop, half expecting that Beatriz would call him with an excuse. He'd canceled a full day of meetings to be here. He'd been so surprised to hear of Beatriz's secret design aspirations. He could hardly believe his luck that he'd found—and so quickly—a way to become her intimate confidante.

Beatriz was wary and fully expecting him to turn on her. He had to earn her trust and convince her that he was in her corner. He had no plans to bring up the lake property or anything relating to it for the time being. Today was all about soothing her fears and stoking her ambitions. The reward—if he ultimately gained it—would be well worth the time and trouble involved.

He climbed out of his car and scanned the street.

To his surprise, Beatriz was already walking toward him, carrying a cardboard cup holder with two cups of coffee and a bag from the pastry shop. She smiled when she saw him. "I brought sustenance. It's a long drive."

He took the coffees and pastries from her. "An excellent idea." He opened the door, and she climbed into the passenger seat of his Audi without a second's hesitation. Her skin glowed and her eyes sparkled, like someone excited to embark on a great adventure.

He walked around and climbed in, then settled their coffees in the cup holders and peered into the bag of pastries. "Mmm, my favorites."

"Eat them all. I had breakfast at the palace before I left." She buckled her seat belt. "The weirdest thing happened in the pastry shop. I ran into my brother Sandro. He never even told us he was coming to Altaleone. Let me just tell my mom he's in town."

He listened to her quick phone call, noticing that she gave no clues as to her whereabouts or plans for the day. Then she hung up and turned off her phone. "Okay, now I'm going ghost on everyone. I don't need them all gabbing about me visiting Milan with you."

"You didn't tell them where I'm taking you?"

"No. I didn't say where I was going or with whom." Her eyes flashed, and a mysterious smile tugged at her mouth. "Better to keep it a secret for now."

"Because of me, or because you don't want them to know you'll soon rival Miucci Prada in fame and fortune?"

"Oh, stop!" She pulled off her gloves. "But you're not exactly the most liked and trusted person in my family."

"Why not?" He barely knew most of them. "They're not hung up on the old family feud are they? That's ancient history."

"I don't think so. I think it was your repeated attempts to secure that land by the lake. It put Darias and Mama on edge."

Hmmm. He thought they had so much land they wouldn't care that much about one remote parcel. Clearly he was wrong. He silently vowed not to repeat the mistake of going through official channels again.

Lorenzo started the engine. "We have an appointment at eleven and my spies tell me the roads are clear between here and Milan, so buckle your seat belt."

She didn't look alarmed but followed his instructions, then picked up her coffee. "I'm glad it didn't snow last night. I was worried something would happen, and we wouldn't be able to go."

She was looking forward to it. That warmed his heart—and somewhere else. Beatriz looked gorgeously severe this morning, as usual, in a black wool coat with black slacks and black boots. He loved her looks—bold and striking won over cherubic cuteness every time with him.

But it wouldn't do to rush things. He was going to need all the restraint he could muster not to rush in and frighten her off. Beatriz was the kind of girl you needed to approach with caution. His best conquests—in business and outside it—had come from careful planning and patient waiting.

Still, it couldn't hurt to build a bridge over the troubled waters that had roiled between their families for centuries. "I miss Rigo. I have yet to encounter a more fearsome tennis opponent."

She laughed. "Rigo's a fearsome opponent in the law too from what I hear. I think he feels he has to be tougher and meaner than everyone so they will take him seriously because he was born a prince."

"I'm sure you're right. He'd hate for people to think he was soft just because he grew up in luxury. But no one can argue with his intelligence. Has he ever lost a case?"

"Never. Last time I spoke to him he told me his latest target had settled out of court just to avoid facing him in a courtroom."

"Do you think he'll ever move back to Altaleone?" They'd now left the village and drove through snowy fields toward the mountains separating Altaleone from northern Italy.

"No." Beatriz sighed. "It's too small for him. New York City is a big enough stage for his grand ambitions. I really should go visit him soon because he never seems to find the time to come back here to visit. I miss his dark sense of humor. Sometimes I think he's the only one who really understands me."

Lorenzo's ears pricked up. "Understands you how?"

She sipped her coffee. "I don't know. People often think I'm a bitch." She glanced at him. "When really I'm just socially awkward or something."

She was testing him. "You're not awkward at all."

"Everyone in my family is so easygoing and warm and sociable. I'm usually most comfortable tucked up in bed with a good book. Rigo and I are the ones who seem to set people's backs up without even trying."

"I admit I haven't met all your brothers and sisters, but so far you and Rigo are my favorites." He winked.

"Obviously you don't like things too easy." She lifted a slim brow.

"*Easy* is often a code word for 'boring.' Who wants to ski down the easy slope?"

"Good point."

4

Beatriz was relieved that the drive was reasonably uneventful. They had a brief wait where an avalanche had temporarily blocked the road on the other side of the mountain, and the snowplows were still pushing the snow around, but after that it was smooth sailing into Milan.

Lorenzo made conversation so easy. His accounts of his travels and his exploits had her laughing so hard that she almost forgot that this man had pursued her, kissed her—albeit only on the hand—then blown her off for six long months.

No sense dwelling on that, though. She was here to see the inner workings of the Milan fashion world and—if all went well—to watch one of her drawings get turned into a real dress. Yes, she was wary that he might try to kiss her.

Or worse, bring up the lake property.

But so far he seemed utterly uninterested in her as either a sexual object or a potential business deal, which was very reassuring.

But if he wasn't interested in getting her into bed or getting his paws on the lake, why had he invited her out to lunch in the first place?

She resolved to enjoy this experience but not to let

her guard down too much around Lorenzo Aldobrando.

Once they arrived in Milan she'd half expected him to take her out for an elegant lunch, but instead they went straight to the atelier. It was up several dusty flights of stairs on the third floor of an old stone building. No sign, no advertising, no glamorous matrons swanning around feeling fabrics between their manicured finger and thumb. Just a big open room with peeling plaster walls, old-fashioned overhead lights and three women—one old and two young, hunched over sewing machines.

None of them looked up as they entered until Lorenzo cleared his throat.

The oldest woman rose to her feet and clapped her hands together. "Signor Aldobrando!" She rushed toward him. "What a pleasure. Your sister told me to expect you." Then she turned to Beatriz with a big smile on her face…that suddenly froze.

Beatriz sighed inwardly. She knew all the signs. She'd been recognized, and this woman was now paralyzed by the fear of doing something wrong and offending a royal.

Beatriz stuck out her hand. "So nice to meet you, Signora…?"

"Pazzi!" the woman hesitated for a second, then wiped her hand on her skirt and offered it. "Emilia Pazzi at your service, your majesty."

"Just Beatriz is fine." She attempted a shaky smile. People had no idea that she found these situations far more awkward than they did. She never seemed to get used to their discomfort or not let it bother her, the way her more easygoing siblings did.

She fumbled in her bag and pulled out her

drawings, suddenly sure that they were going to be all wrong and that no one on earth could possibly see how to turn them into a wearable garment.

Signora Pazzi pushed a pair of reading glasses onto her nose and studied them. Her lips moved as she flipped from one to the next. Beatriz had brought the drawing she'd originally shown Lorenzo, and two new ones, of the back and side view.

"Is there enough detail?" asked Beatriz, nervous at the long silence. "Do you think the neckline is too asymmetrical or that there's too much fabric at the hem?"

Signora Pazzi lifted her eyes from the drawings, pushed her reading glasses up into her salt and pepper hair and turned her steely gaze on Beatriz. "Please take off your coat."

Beatriz shrugged out of it, and Lorenzo took it from her. She'd worn a simple black cashmere sweater and black trousers. It was risky to strive for style when coming to the fashion capital of Europe. She preferred to retreat into safe classics.

The dressmaker looked her up and down, from her shoulders to her waist. Beatriz held herself steady, trying not to show fear. Was Signora Pazzi assessing the dismal smallness of her chest or the thickness of her waist? Or perhaps she could see her shapeless piano legs even through the drape of her slacks? At moments like this any cruel comment casually made in the media came back to haunt her.

Was she going to say something that would humiliate her in front of Lorenzo and make her wish she'd never been stupid enough to come here? Why on earth had she agreed to be the model for her own dress? "If you think it would make more sense to tailor the dress for someone else, I'm totally on board with that."

Signora Pazzi looked confused. "Someone else? Oh, no. It will be perfect on you. Let me get my tape."

Beatriz tried not to breathe, or sweat, while the seamstress measured every inch of her body. She could feel Lorenzo's gaze on her—he thought she was too preoccupied to notice—and it made her hyperaware of every slight twitch of her muscles or even her eyelashes.

"Once she's taken your measurements she can make you anything," said Lorenzo. "You could just call up and say, 'I'd like a hot pink parachute jumpsuit,' and she can have it ready by that afternoon. Right, signora? Steffi told me she did that once with a pirate costume she needed for a party."

Signora Pazzi tutted. "Only if I have the materials on hand." She looked up at Beatriz. "If I have to shop for the materials it takes an additional day."

"That's very impressive."

"I took the liberty of bringing in some fabrics for this dress." Her language was stilted enough that Beatriz knew she was still a bit uncomfortable around her.

"Fantastic. How thoughtful."

"Of course I only had Mr. Aldobrando's description to go on. He said silver and needed to drape well. So I picked up some shantung and some charmeuse." She jotted down the last measurement, threw her tape around her neck and tucked her pen behind her ear. Then she walked to the other side of the room, where a scarred wood table was piled high with bolts of silver-gray fabric in every shade from dark charcoal to a sparkling white satin.

Signora Pazzi turned and stared at her expectantly. *I have to choose.* She decided to act with the confidence the seamstress seemed to expect of her, rifling through the bolts, looking for the fabric that most closely matched the image in her mind. She pulled out a bolt of pale silver charmeuse with only a very slight sheen to it. "This."

"Beautiful." Signora Pazzi clapped her hands together again. "Give me an hour and we'll be ready for the first fitting."

Beatriz's eyes widened. "Today?" She hadn't really planned to strip down to her underwear today. Though she should have expected this after Lorenzo's enthusiastic endorsement of the seamstress's speed. And was Lorenzo going to stand there and watch?

It was the dead of winter, and her skin was pallid and sad-looking. And she hadn't been getting as much exercise now that her dad was gone. Some days it took all her energy just to go out to the stables and ride her horse in the indoor arena. This seamstress was used to dressing models and she was anything but…

"We'll go find some lunch, and then we'll come back." Lorenzo beamed with confidence. If he was gleefully anticipating seeing her almost naked after lunch, he'd be sorely disappointed. She resolved then and there to ask him to wait outside, even if he was paying for this whole adventure.

Her head was still spinning as she walked back down the flights of stairs. "See," he said, his deep voice startling her from her reveries. "I told you I'd find someone who knows what she's doing. Steffi says she's the best seamstress in Milan. She can even run off an exact copy of any designer original just from looking at a photo of it. Not that Steffi would ever order that kind of thing, of course."

She glanced back to see his cheeky grin. "Thank Steffi for her trouble in finding someone."

"No trouble at all. Steffi and I both thoroughly enjoy the world of fashion. We're usually looking for ways to become involved in it."

"You? I'm surprised."

"You think that only gay men enjoy fashion?" His gray eyes flashed a challenge.

"No. I suppose not. I guess it's just not what I expected."

"You said that people don't see the real you. Perhaps I have the same problem." He lifted a brow. "People only see what they expect to see."

They'd reached the door at the bottom of the stairs and pushed back out into the frosty sunlight. "You have a point," she admitted. Maybe there as a lot more to Lorenzo Aldobrando than his rather dubious reputation as a wheeler-dealer from a family of shady—if wealthy and established—characters. "I'll give you the benefit of the doubt. For now."

He laughed. "I like how you don't mince words, Beatriz."

"That's refreshing too. Most people wish I would mince them more often."

"I think some hot, freshly made pasta is in order. Does that sound good?"

"It sounds perfect."

Lunch was wonderful—as could be expected at one of Milan's finest restaurants, which was only a couple of blocks walk from the atelier. She checked her phone as they waited for their appetizers, and saw that her mom had called. Her mom would have a heart attack if she knew who her daughter was with right now. Most likely she just wanted to know what Darias said about the business cards, but that was hardly an urgent matter.

It occurred to her that she knew nothing about Lorenzo's family. "Do your mother and father live in Italy?"

His gray eyes darkened. "My father lived on the family estate near Torino but he passed away last year. My mother died sixteen years ago."

She instantly regretted asking. "I'm so sorry."

"I'm not. He was angry at the world since the day she died. Maybe he's happier now."

She blinked in surprise. It was hard to imagine being happy that your father was dead when she missed hers so much.

"He was a very difficult man," Lorenzo said, almost apologetic. "Very demanding. My friends tell me that's why I'm so driven and why I work so hard. Like I'm still trying to impress him even though he's dead."

"Do you think that's true?"

Humor twinkled in his gaze. "Maybe. Or maybe I just don't know how to live any other way. Work hard, play hard, that's what I was raised to do."

"My father was all about playing hard. Not so much the work," said Beatriz with a smile. "He enjoyed life so much. I miss hunting with him."

"I'd love to go hunting with you."

"Really?" Beatriz couldn't quite picture Lorenzo sitting on a horse for hours while hounds sniffed around in the bushes. "Because I haven't been once since he died. There's excellent hunting around the lake. In fact that's the only reason we ever went there."

Lorenzo leaned in. "I haven't been hunting in years. My father thought it was a waste of time. He only encouraged me to go on a few hunts because he considered it part of a gentleman's education, like learning how to sail and play tennis."

"I've always wanted to learn to sail."

"I keep a small boat in Chiogga. I take it down to the Greek islands at least once every summer. You'll have to come with me this year."

Beatriz's eyes widened. "That sounds amazing."

His smile caused the most adorable crinkle lines around his eyes. "I think maybe I need to work less, and play more."

"That sounds like an excellent plan." Her brother Darias phoned while they were sipping coffee after their meal. She ignored it, and decided to turn her phone right off again. Surely her family could just talk among themselves for one afternoon? They was so used to assuming that she had nothing but time on her hands and was available to run their errands or listen to their minor problems at the drop of a hat.

And right now she was having way too much fun to worry about them. It felt great to step out and spend the day doing something unexpected and exciting—with a man who was turning out to be equally surprising and intriguing.

After lunch they strolled through some high-end boutiques and shared opinions on the season's looks. Beatriz thoroughly enjoyed being able to share her thoughts about different styles and shapes with someone who didn't think her ideas were pointless nonsense but who actually understood and could engage in discussion about the finer points of design.

Perhaps people noticed and recognized her, but no one said anything. And there was a secret thrill in being seen about town with such a handsome and dashing man. She noticed that he attracted female attention wherever they went, yet his eyes never wandered. If Lorenzo Aldobrando intended to get her under his spell, it was working.

After about two hours they headed back to the atelier. The buzz from her lunchtime glass of wine had started to wear off, and the nerves—perhaps fuelled by strong coffee—started to kick in.

Her heart thudded as they climbed the stairs, and she tried to visualize her creation made out of fabric, rather than simply pencil and dreams.

The dress was pinned onto a mannequin at one end of the studio, sewn but not yet hemmed or lined. No doubt that came after it was expertly fitted.

She undressed behind a standing fabric screen, and the seamstress brought the dress back there and helped her into it. Signora Pazzi's careful measuring and expertise had produced a near-perfect fit.

"I should have brought heels," she murmured when she noticed how the hem dragged on the floor. "Just stand on your tiptoes," said the seamstress in a conspiratorial whisper. "The dress looks good on you."

Does it? Beatriz wanted to see herself in the big mirror at the far end of the studio, but that meant stepping out in front of Lorenzo Aldobrando's appraising gaze. This time he might be critiquing not only her personal appearance but also the artistry of her design.

She drew in a breath—slowly and carefully so as

not to put pressure on the seams—and stepped out from behind the screen.

Her eyes flew to Lorenzo's. He raked his gaze down over her—permissible under the circumstances but still disconcerting—and she watched as a smile lifted one corner of his mouth. His eyes met hers. "Beautiful. The fabric is perfect." He gestured toward the mirror for her to take a look.

She hardly dared lift her eyes, but when she did she saw herself walking, rather awkwardly on tiptoe, so as not to drag the hem on the floor, with the smooth silvery silk draping over her thighs as she moved.

Damn. It does look good. As she'd hoped, the silk draped elegantly over her form without clinging, and the asymmetry of the neck and hemline added quiet drama that made her look taller and more shapely than she actually was.

She glanced at Signora Pazzi and could almost swear she saw a smile in the older woman's eyes, even though her mouth was pursed in stern appraisal. "A little tighter under the armpits, I think," she muttered.

"Perhaps a millimeter or two," agreed Beatriz, "but overall you cut it perfectly."

"It's a magnificent dress." Lorenzo walked toward her. "And I've never seen anything quite like it. Elegant and unexpected at the same time." His gaze rested on hers for a moment. "Like its designer."

"Oh, stop." She drew in a shaky breath. "I feel self-conscious enough already. But, Signora Pazzi, you did a wonderful job. And so fast!"

Signora Pazzi put in a couple of pins under the armholes where the fabric needed to be taken in by a few millimeters. "Are there any other adjustments you'd like me to make?"

"None. It's exactly as I imagined. You've literally made my dream come true." Beatriz couldn't stop a goofy grin sneaking across her face as she looked her creation up and down in the mirror. How many of these sketches had she done over the years—five hundred? Maybe even a thousand. And she never expected to see one come to life in silver-gray silk, let alone see it draped expertly over her own body.

Which looked pretty damn good in it, truth be told!

Lorenzo grinned. She could tell he was pleased that his plan was a success. "How long will it take to finish the dress?"

"Another hour for the adjustments, hem and partial lining," said Signora Pazzi. "It will be ready for pickup by four."

"Excellent. We'll go entertain ourselves for a while."

Beatriz dressed and they headed back downstairs. Beatriz turned her phone back on—she shouldn't go incommunicado all day—as they stepped out into the crispy, icy afternoon.

"Shall we go to a museum? There's an interesting exhibit of contemporary textile artists at the—"

Beatriz stared as her phone came to life and revealed that she'd missed twelve calls and had seven voice mail messages. Why would she get so many calls in such a short period? Before she even had time to call her voice mail, the phone rang. Her brother Sandro. This time she answered, nerves already tightening in anticipation.

"Hello?"

"Beatriz! We're all frantic about you. Mom's been

trying to call you."

"Why?" The edge in his voice made her anxiety ratchet higher.

"There's been a...development." He hesitated. "Something awful arrived in the mail. Why didn't you answer?"

She swallowed. She didn't want anyone to know where she'd been today. "I was busy."

"Who are you with?"

And she certainly didn't want them to know she was out with Lorenzo. "Is it really any of your business? I don't question your every movement and quiz you about your companions."

She regretted how snappy she sounded, but this inquisition made her nervous. She tried to take one single lousy afternoon off to do something that meant a lot to her and now she was being treated like a murder suspect.

"Can you come home now? It was some kind of threat."

"What?" Terror spiked through her.

"Gibran is investigating, but he wants us all safely under guard here at the palace. I'm here myself, with Serena."

"Oh." The fear gripping her chest eased a little. Just a threat. If anything really bad had happened he would have said. But clearly they didn't like her being off somewhere by herself. As usual she was being treated like the baby of the family when she was actually the oldest of them all. Still, she wasn't going to leave them hanging. She didn't want to upset her mom. "I'll be back soon. Bye."

Damn. This was the end of her magical afternoon. And she wouldn't get to see the dress finished, either.

Another episode in the anticlimactic life of Beatriz Leone.

"Lorenzo…" Her voice sounded flat. She was letting him down as well, after all he'd done today. "I'm afraid I need to go home right now."

5

Beatriz found herself on edge all evening. Her father's and grandmother's bodies had been stolen from the family graveyard despite the constant presence of armed guards, and Gibran, the security chief, suspected it was an inside job.

Worse yet, her beloved father's finger had been severed and sent to her mom in the post. What kind of sadist would do such a horrible thing? It turned her stomach to think about it.

If that wasn't bad enough, everyone wanted to know where she'd been all day and with who—and why—when it was none of their business. The inquisition started as they were about to go in for dinner. Sandro's new girlfriend Serena was admiring her mom's gold necklace with an intricate pattern of interwoven vines.

Beatriz loved the necklace and immediately liked Serena all the more for noticing it. "We had a jeweler appraise it three years ago, and he said it likely dates back to the Byzantine era, and may even have belonged to Empress Theodora." Serena looked appropriately dazzled, and Beatriz was about to share an interesting tidbit about Theodora's renowned jewelery collection when Darias rudely interrupted her.

"Fascinating, Beatriz, but stop trying to distract us with trivia and tell us where you were all day."

Beatriz struggled to keep her composure. She did not want them to know she was out with Lorenzo. Darias would tease her mercilessly like he always had on the rare occasions she actually had a date of any kind. "I simply went for a drive."

"Taking two coffees and a bag of pastries with you," said Sandro.

"Exactly." She lifted her chin. "It takes a lot of caffeine and calories to keep me going when it's this cold."

"I can relate to that," said Serena.

Beatriz warmed to her even further. "See? Finally someone else here understands. It's nice to see you again, Serena." Then a distraction technique occurred to her. "I hope they didn't put you in the moonlight room." The room was famously haunted. Though none of them had ever seen a ghost, their guests occasionally had a sleepless night there.

"Why?"

"Oh, stop it, Beatriz," said her mom. "You know there's nothing wrong with that room. It's one of the nicest. And it's right next to Sandro's."

"Oh, yes. I'd forgotten about that." They probably wanted to sneak into each other's rooms at night. And why not?

Still, her distraction was working. And she suddenly thought of a way to up the ante and get back at Darias for years of teasing all at the same time. Her heart beat faster as she resolved to reveal a secret she'd been keeping for some time now. "But no one can argue that strange things happen in that room. I swear a voice told me to look on top of the big armoire one afternoon, so I pulled up a chair, and found the strangest thing up there."

"What were you doing in there in the first place?" asked Darias gruffly.

"Oh, it was right before the coronation. I think I was just making sure it was set up to receive guests after Emma moved out."

"Surely the servants could have taken care of that," continued Darias, looking increasingly wary. Beatriz felt a rare thrill of victory. It was nice to see her bossy brother on the defensive for a change.

"Aren't you going to ask what I found up there?" Beatriz lifted a brow.

"I think I know what you found," said Emma, her voice quiet.

Beatriz hesitated for a moment. She liked Emma very much. Still, she wasn't about to reveal anything they didn't already know. "I bet you do. And since it's common knowledge now that my brother paid you to marry him—for one year—it will come as no surprise to anyone here that there was a contract detailing the particulars of the arrangement. That's what I found on top of the armoire."

She looked at Darias, who looked appropriately chastened for about half a second. It really wasn't fair that he should do something so underhanded and end up with such a lovely and sweet wife as Emma. Everything Darias touched turned to gold. She cocked a brow. "The year isn't up yet."

Darias was never fazed by her biting humor. He simply put his arm around Emma's waist and squeezed her close. "Emma and I have long since moved past that. My urgent need to find a wife in time for the coronation proved to be the best thing that ever happened to me." Then he kissed Emma so sweet and slow that even Beatriz felt her chest tighten with emotion.

He loves her so much, that bastard brother of mine. Why would he begrudge me the same happiness? Maybe she and Lorenzo would hold each other affectionately like that one day, in full view of the whole family.

But only if she didn't let Darias—or anyone else— crush her budding romance before it even had a chance to blossom.

"It was my fault it was up there." Emma's cheeks were now pink. "I should never have brought it here with me. I'm not even sure why I did. And when I moved into Darias's bedroom after the wedding I forgot it was up there. Then a coronation guest moved into the room and I wasn't able to retrieve it. When I finally found the time to sneak back in there, it was gone." She blinked. "I'm glad it was you who found it, Beatriz. I was worried it might get leaked to the press."

"I'm the very soul of discretion." Beatriz winked so that only Emma could see her. She hoped that Emma could tell what she was doing. She'd thrown her under the bus but only as a very effective strategy to divert attention from her own activities. She was pretty sure Emma would understand when she explained it to her one day.

"All right, everyone." Her mom was clearly ready to move on. "Let's go in to dinner."

Dinner was exhausting, as Beatriz seized every opportunity to focus the conversation on anyone except herself. Aunt Liesel arrived near the end of dinner, hot off a flight from Germany. Beatriz had called her earlier and told her about the bodies. She knew Liesel would come—Liesel could never resist family drama—and Beatriz had quietly encouraged her just to keep her mom occupied so she wouldn't quiz Beatriz about where she was all afternoon when they were trying to reach her.

Couldn't she have been allowed just one perfect afternoon before returning to her dreary duties as the boring spinster sister?

No. Apparently not. And now she was forced to bluster and tell half truths so no one would freak out over her spending time with Lorenzo Aldobrando.

She finally managed to excuse herself and head up to bed when she overheard Sandro talking to Serena on the other side of the archway.

"I don't know what's eating my sister Beatriz. She's not usually like that. Something's got her back up."

Too right. No wonder she never managed to have a proper relationship, living in this fishbowl of interfering busybodies, with far too many brothers each of whom had a strong—usually negative— opinion about any man she even spoke to. Well, this time was going to be different.

Alone in her room she itched to call Lorenzo but apprehension overcame her as she picked up her phone. What if he was busy? She didn't want to seem pushy. Instead she texted him. **Sorry I had to leave early. I enjoyed today.**

As soon as she'd sent it, her text seemed bland and disappointing. Like her.

Not as much as me. It was a thrill seeing your creation come to life. And even better getting to spend time with you. Would you like to go skiing

tomorrow?

She blinked at his response. He still wanted to see her again? The prospect sent a thrill of anticipation through her.

He hadn't mentioned the lake property even once. Maybe he wasn't just trying to warm her up so he could get his hands on it. But she couldn't accept an invitation so quickly either. He'd know she was desperate.

Can't, sorry. Have to ride my horse. Her big baby didn't do well with anyone else on him. Matteo was a good rider but too firm with Gatto, and if Gatto went more than two days without being ridden he got wound up.

I'd like to ride with you.

She drew in a breath. Lorenzo was an excellent rider. She'd watched him manage an unknown horse with ease in the cramped space of a palace courtyard during the joust at the coronation.

Not tomorrow. Things are tense here. Can't say more right now.

It wasn't a good idea to encourage him. Whatever was going on between them—and she wasn't at all sure what it was—couldn't go anywhere. Rigo aside, her family was deeply suspicious of his family and vice versa. Her mom had already warned her about him and told her to stay away from him, and her mom was truly her best friend and the warmest, kindest person she knew.

I'll pick up the dress tomorrow and find a way to get it to you.

Was he really going to drive all the way back to Milan himself? Unlikely. He'd send a messenger or have it delivered. Still, it was sweet of him to think of it after she'd ruined the climax of his carefully planned day.

That's very kind of you. I have to go now. Good night.

She had to end this text conversation. It was rattling her already raw nerves. She felt like Lorenzo was there in the bedroom with her and might show up in her dreams, which would be disturbing.

Goodnight, Beatriz.

And that was it. She let out a sigh, wishing she could breathe away the tension built up inside her. She couldn't even remember the last time she'd been interested in a man. Usually if one even spoke to her she could rattle off at least three reasons why he was trying to curry favor with her father or one of her brothers or gain royal favor for his company.

She'd certainly had the same suspicions about Lorenzo Aldobrando. But after today…maybe he really did like her?

It seemed unlikely, given that he was rich and handsome and must have girls trailing after him. But then she was a princess. And she did own the lake house he'd shown such intense interest in.

See? Even now she didn't imagine for one second that it was she herself who attracted Lorenzo. Most likely she was just a stepping-stone to somewhere else, and she'd do best to focus on helping her family through this difficult time.

She felt bad that they'd been so worried about her—all because she'd turned her phone off to escape from them. What kind of person did that make her? And she'd shut them out because of Lorenzo Aldobrando.

He'd made her temporarily take leave of her

senses.

Her family were the most important people in her world, and her duty to them came first, and she'd better keep that in mind.

The next day, Beatriz was in the indoor arena, cantering Gatto over a small course of jumps, when her phone rang inside her jacket. She slowed her horse and pulled her phone out and saw the cryptic "L" she'd typed into her contacts.

Adrenaline rushed through her. "Hello?"

"Beatriz, I have the dress. I'll bring it by the palace."

"No!" She said it so fast it sounded rude. "Don't do that."

"Do you not want anyone to see me?" He sounded curious rather than offended.

She swallowed. "Something like that. We have a big staff, and they talk a lot. The cook saw me getting into your car yesterday. They'd been speculating all day about where I was. I don't want to fuel that fire."

"But what is wrong about me seeing you?"

She hesitated. She didn't really want to tell him how much her family seemed to dislike him. Him trying—twice—to lease the lake property had made Darias very wary of him. "My family's just a bit weird. And right now they're paranoid because..." She'd been told to keep the stolen bodies and grisly package secret. "Because of the murders."

"That was last year."

She felt a burst of exasperation. "Lorenzo, someone killed my father and grandmother. It's not going away."

"I understand. I'm sorry. I'd love to see you."

Gatto's hot breath made white steam against the cold air of the indoor riding arena. "I'd like to see you too," she admitted, as quietly as she could. There was only one groom left since her dad had died and his horses been sold or retired, but he could be nearby.

"We could meet in town."

She'd been told not to go anywhere—even into town—without a security escort in light of recent events, but her guard—a woman called Nina—should be easy to dodge if she said she was going to the stables. She was only supposed to follow Beatriz if she actually left the palace grounds. The staff entrance to the stables would put her on a narrow side lane that ran along the outside of the palace wall and led right into a small wood on the edge of town.

"Okay. Do you know the woods at the end of Locarno Street?"

"I know where they are."

"Meet me there in half an hour. Just come into the woods and I'll find you."

"I'll look for a trail of bread crumbs," he teased. "See you there."

Beatriz tucked her phone away and realized she had a huge grin on her face. She wiped it off and reached down to pat Gatto. His broad dark bay neck and black mane had absorbed a lot of her tears over the past few months. "Am I making a huge mistake, Gatto?"

She jumped down and lifted the reins over his big head. She only had half an hour to change and creep out of the palace. She fed Gatto his carrots, then handed him to Matteo, the groom. She also asked him to clean her saddle immediately. He might find that imperious behavior, but it would keep him busy while she crept past him and out of the stables.

Excitement trickled through her at the prospect of seeing Lorenzo, and she cursed herself for it. Why? She was hardly going to try her new dress on in the woods. So she must be excited about seeing *him*.

Which sucked because it was bound to end in tears.

She smiled briskly at Nina and told her she could relax before heading into the shower, then dressed in dark pants, a sweater and a jacket as if she were just going for a walk around the grounds. She was tempted to ask her brother's girlfriend if she could borrow her adorable black-and-white dog—that would be a nice excuse for a stroll—but after Beatriz's performance last night Serena probably wouldn't trust her with her precious pooch.

She hurried along the back corridors, then down the brick arches of the stable block. This area used to bustle with life and activity when her dad was still out hunting four days a week. It was still hard to believe—devastating, in fact—that would never happen again.

She slunk around the edges of the rectangular stable yard, staying out of view, then exited through the side door gate that used to allow horse-drawn tradesmen traffic in and out of the palace. It wasn't guarded because the lane behind it had been out of use for nearly a century, except by riders. The track led over a meadow and down a short hill, then into the woods by the town.

She'd ridden the route many times, but today she felt a weird sense of unease that made her glance backward. She couldn't shake the feeling that she was being watched. That she was doing something wrong. Perhaps because she knew the family wouldn't like her going out alone after yesterday's events.

And that they wouldn't like her meeting Lorenzo.

Just last night she'd resolved to stick by her family and forget about Lorenzo, but all it took was one phone call and she was sneaking off to meet him. Was this normal behavior for an adult woman?

Before her lay untrodden fresh snow, and behind her the old stone wall that surrounded the palace grounds. It was too high for anyone to peer over, and there was no one coming or going on the snowy track. So why did she feel like eyes were everywhere?

The snow came almost to the top of her boots. Anyone wishing to track her movements would have no trouble following her footsteps in the pristine white landscape. Even the cows were inside for the winter. As she crested the top of the meadow and looked down at the town in the valley on the other side, she felt like a sitting target.

But who would want her dead? She was the Leone that no one even remembered.

She headed down toward the woods. The snow on the trees had blown off, leaving them dark and forbidding against the bright landscape. She hurried toward the cover of their branches, eager to be out of sight from the palace. Inside the wood were well-groomed trails where villagers walked their dogs and couples met to kiss inside the leafy sanctuary.

Her nerves jangled as she thought of kissing. Lorenzo had stolen that kiss from her at the coronation, then seemingly forgotten all about her. Should she be relieved or discouraged that he didn't even attempt to kiss her yesterday?

Perhaps he would have tried if she hadn't rushed home unexpectedly.

She pulled her collar up around her ears as she walked from the sunny field into the shady depths of the woods. The trees were mostly evergreen and cast long shadows in the low winter sun.

She pulled out her phone and texted Lorenzo. **I'm here.**

The woods were small, less than five hectares, but it was still possible to miss someone due to the winding paths and poor visibility. Her phone pinged.

Me too.

Her nerves prickled with excitement.

Until she realized that the text wasn't from Lorenzo. She stopped in her tracks as she noticed that although she'd sent her text to Lorenzo, the one coming into her phone was from an unknown number.

An icy finger of fear clawed down her spine. Should she turn and run back to the palace? Or was that marking herself as prey? She'd have to cross at least four hundred yards of open country before she'd reach the safety of the castle wall.

She glanced about, unable to see anyone for the thick forest.

Maybe it was Lorenzo, and her phone was acting up. Yes. That was it. He must have two lines. She needed to stop freaking out and overreacting to everything.

Where are you?
Right behind you.

6

She spun around, and a tiny cry rose in her throat when there was no one there.

Heart pounding, she spun wildly, looking around her in a panic. "Lorenzo!" she cried. Had he even received her texts, or had someone intercepted them?

"Beatriz!" His disembodied voice reached her through the trees. Thank heaven! "Say my name again, so I can find you."

"Lorenzo," she said aloud, looking all around her. She could kill him for scaring her like this. What a jerk! "I'm right here,"

He appeared along a path to her right, striding forward, wearing a long camel coat and carrying a black shopping bag. The grin on his handsome face both excited and infuriated her.

"You almost scared me to death," she admitted. "I need an apology."

He frowned. "For what? I'm not even late."

"Don't play dumb with me." She raised a brow. At least he hadn't tried to kiss her or anything. "It's really not funny given what's going on at the palace."

Lorenzo stared at her, confusion in his gray eyes. "What's not funny?"

"The texts! *I'm behind you.* I almost had a heart

attack."

"I didn't text you back yet. I just got your texts saying that you're here and asking where I was. I was just about to text you back when I heard you call my name." He took a step toward her, concern on his face, as if he was worried about her sanity.

"This joke has gone on long enough." She turned her phone to him. "Ha ha ha."

He moved right up to her and took her phone. Then he glanced up and scanned the woods. "I didn't send these."

Her heart clenched. "What?"

He handed her phone back and pulled out his own. He showed her his recent text messages and sure enough her two texts were there—but no replies.

"So you got them, but someone else responded?" She scanned the dark woods. There was no sign of anyone. "How is that even possible? This doesn't make any sense. Why would someone…?"

"Someone is trying to scare you." He took her phone back. "And they know where you are. Let's go." He slid his arm around her waist and pulled her along the path he'd come on. "Let's head into town, where there are people around."

"I shouldn't have left the palace without a guard." She didn't want to tell him about what happened yesterday. The whole family had agreed to keep it secret for now, so only those involved in the criminal acts would know—and might reveal themselves through their knowledge.

In less that five minutes they emerged from the woods onto the manicured and snow-cleared lawn of the town park, surrounded by the reassuring rooftops of the village and the sight of people pushing their babies in prams and walking their dogs.

"I'm totally creeped out."

"I suspect that's the intention." Lorenzo's arm was still at her waist. It made her feel safer. At least no one would shoot at her, or try to abduct her, with him literally wrapped around her. "Bastards. I wish I knew who it was." He scanned the streets. "My car's right here."

"I'm not sure I should go anywhere." She'd been told not to go into town alone, let alone drive out of it. "I didn't tell anyone I was going out."

"You're a grown-up, aren't you?" He looked amused.

"Yes, but...I can't really say what's going on, but things are dangerous right now."

And I still came out alone to see you.

Did he know how much power he had over her right now?

"Well, I'm not letting you walk back to the palace alone, so we can go somewhere, or I'll take you back there. Your choice. I think you should go to the police."

She bit her lip. "I'll tell the palace staff when I get back. But not yet." She had a feeling that if they saw her with Lorenzo she'd never hear the end of it.

And it would be the end of her ever seeing him again.

"Let's go to the Orangerie," she said quickly. "It's a smaller house my dad used to use sometimes. It's just outside town on Steiner Street, and no one goes there anymore."

His eyes narrowed. "What about your family? Won't they miss you?"

"They'll just think I'm at the stables or in another

part of the palace. That's an advantage of living in a place bigger than many neighborhoods."

"If you're sure." They'd reached his car, and he held the passenger door open for her.

"I'm sure." She wanted to see the dress almost as much as she wanted more time with him.

Lorenzo climbed in beside her. Dark jeans encased his muscled legs today. His leather-gloved hand gripped the gearshift as they pulled out of his space. Adrenaline rippled through her. "Maybe the texts were someone playing a prank. My brother Sandro's visiting, and he can be a bit of a joker." Unlikely but not impossible.

"Try texting back. Ask what they want." Sandro drove through the narrow streets.

Beatriz hesitated. Sitting next to Lorenzo gave her confidence. She pulled out her phone and typed, **You're not behind me right now.** "Let's see if they respond."

They waited while an old lady walked her dog slowly across the road in front of the car.

No, but I will be again soon.

An icy finger of fear raked down her spine. She read the text aloud, hating the way her voice shook.

Who are you? she typed, determined not to be cowed into silence. The answer came almost right away.

Your worst nightmare.

Lorenzo glanced at her phone, then up at her. "What is your worst nightmare?"

She blinked. "Probably being murdered like my dad or my grandma." This time she couldn't hide the tears in her voice.

Lorenzo pulled the car into an empty space on a

side street, unbuckled his seat belt and wrapped his arms around her. "I won't let anything happen to you."

His big, warm embrace made her almost believe him.

After a few moments she could breathe again. "Are you going to follow me everywhere?" she teased.

"I'd like that very much." His sexy mouth hitched on one side.

"Don't you have work to do?"

"My schedule is flexible." He lifted a brow slightly. His gray eyes locked onto hers, warmth dancing in their depths. "Any time you need me, I'll be there."

His voice was deeper than usual and gave his words a tone of gruff honesty that made him sound utterly convincing. Even though she knew it was impossible, something stirred inside her and she felt more cared for than she had since...since her father was taken from her.

And there was the desire. It surged low in her belly and rose up through her, loosening her muscles. Lorenzo had a powerful effect on her. She heard his breathing deepen. He could feel it too—that gave her a strange sense of reassurance.

"Tell me the way to the Orangerie." He pulled back from her with obvious reluctance. "Because I want to get there as fast as possible."

Half smiling, she gave him directions. It was less than five minutes away. "I hope they haven't changed the code," she said as they pulled up. Her dad refused to ever change lock codes because he couldn't remember the new ones and hated having to ask the staff. "Pull up to the gate, and I'll get out and try it."

She got out and walked around to the driver's side and tapped it in. The gate started to creak open. "We put some guests up here for the coronation months ago, but as far as I know it's been empty since."

The gate opened into a cobbled courtyard once used for horses. There were stables on one side the courtyard, on the other two sides was the house—which wasn't an orangerie at all but might have once had one built next to it. The town had since crept up onto the original eighteenth-century grounds of which her ancestors had granted parcels to local grandees to build their in-town houses.

Her father had kept this very private house as a retreat from the palace. There were no staff, except someone who cleaned once a week or so. Her brother Rigo had once crudely suggested that he had affairs here, but she chose not to believe it. She'd had the code ever since one afternoon when her dad had asked her to bring him some papers here, and he wouldn't want her to surprise him if he was cheating, would he?

She used the same code to unlock the green door. Lorenzo closed it and locked it behind them. "Don't need anyone following us in," he said, lifting the black bag with the dress in it.

"Please, let me see it." She took the bag with a prickle of anxiety. "I'm nervous. What if it looks terrible?"

"You've already seen it in progress so you know it won't."

She sighed. "Here goes nothing. Why don't you stay here?" She gestured to a white sofa. The house looked more like a normal house than the other royal residences, with its intimate eighteenth-century proportions and cozy rooms.

She went into the room next door, another sitting room with a fireplace and a large, framed mirror, and quickly disrobed down to her underwear. She took her bra off so the straps wouldn't ruin the outline of the neck.

The silk dress felt cool and magical in her hands. She lifted it up over her head and let it cascade down over her, caressing her body like a lover. She'd designed it to fit and hug without zippers, and she was still surprised by how perfectly it fit.

She looked up slowly, half afraid to see her reflection in the mirror. Her frown startled her, and she made an effort to wipe it away. Then she looked at the dress. Perfect! She was no model, but it made her almost look like one. She pulled her hair from its tight bun and let it cascade down her back.

Much better. Now she smiled at herself.

Better yet. She inhaled a deep breath and watched the fabric tighten against her aroused nipples.

"Are you ready yet?" Lorenzo's impatient call from the other room made her chuckle.

"Yes, come in."

She held her breath, afraid half of his reaction to her and half of her reaction to him. She was already aroused from close proximity and the way he'd made her feel safe after her scare.

He opened the door and stopped to stare. Naturally she expected his eyes to drop to her body and examine the dress, maybe ripping it apart mentally like a critic, or even analyzing the flaws in her body that undermined the design.

But his gaze rested on her face. He was more interested in her reaction—how she felt—than how the dress looked. "Are you happy with it?"

She shrugged, suddenly afraid to praise her own work. "What do you think?"

Now he let his gaze drift lower, roaming over her shoulders, then down to where the bodice gently hugged her breasts, lower to where the silk cascaded over her hips and down to the asymmetrical hemline. "I like it."

She laughed. She'd expected some florid adjective like *fabulous* and been prepared to assume it was phony, so his simple praise caught her by surprise.

"Me too." She smiled, feeling shy. "Signora Pazzi did a great job."

Lorenzo walked toward her, eyes still appraising the dress. "She did what she does every day. Your design reveals your talent. Are you sure you've never studied fashion?"

Her nipples tightened under the cool silk as she felt his eyes graze over them. "I've studied it since I was little by poring over fashion magazines. I've just never taken a class in fashion design."

"You don't need to. This dress demonstrates that you know what you're doing." His face showed admiration that echoed his words.

She shrugged, feeling shy and proud at the same time. "It's exciting to see something that I imagined come to life." She swallowed. "Thank you."

"You're more than welcome." His gaze rested on her, expectant.

She didn't know what to say. "I guess the big question is when I should wear it."

He cocked his head. "I think the far more important question is can you have the rest of the collection ready for fashion week this spring?"

"What?"

"You heard me." He regarded her steadily, his gaze challenging. "It gives you almost three months to get the drawings done, the samples sewn, the venue booked and the guests invited."

She laughed. "I'm not a real designer."

His warm gray gaze drifted down her body. "I beg to differ. I think you'll be the talk of Milan this spring."

She blinked. "I can see the headlines already. 'Spoiled Princess Thinks She's a Designer.'"

"No way. You don't even have to tell people it's you. You could use a brand name. Then when they're all oohing and ahhing over your designs you reveal the truth."

She inhaled slowly. Could she? She loved the idea of surprising anyone who'd mocked her dream over the years. Not that she'd even brought it up more than five times. Her dad had squashed the idea before it got to the discussion phase.

But he was gone now.

Guilt suddenly racked her. "I think it would be disrespectful to my dad."

Lorenzo frowned. "I'm sure he'd be thrilled to see you pursue your dream. He never had any idea how much it meant to you."

She bit her lip. "He thought it was foolish. Perhaps because my siblings are geniuses. Callista's a scientist on the verge of a big breakthrough in genetics, Rigo's a top lawyer, Sandro developed a new kind of solar panel…"

"Uh, your brother Darias—who is now the king, I might add—paints pictures of nude women."

She laughed. "They're very well-respected pictures.

They sell for hundreds of thousands each. Besides, my dad always hated that Darias painted. He forbade him to do it many times. Darias was just too damn stubborn to quit."

Lorenzo grinned. "Then you need to take a page out of his book."

She stared at him. The dress—her own design that fit her perfectly—suddenly felt like just the armor she'd need for such an undertaking. "My grandmother left me some money. I could use that, and no one would know."

"And I bet your grandmother would be pleased to know you put it to good use."

Beatriz smiled. "She would. She was always a bit of a maverick—in secret. She became queen when she was quite young so she told me she learned to sneak her fun in without people noticing."

Her grandmother had told Beatriz about two torrid affairs she'd managed to engage in—with thoroughly unsuitable men—before settling down to an officially sanctioned marriage.

"That settles it. Lets get your drawings to Signora Pazzi as soon as possible."

"But I need to do new ones! I can't just bring out a bunch of old drawings and call them a collection. I need to come up with a theme and design everything as part of it."

"You're the expert." He grinned again. "So just tell me what I need to do to help."

She turned and looked at herself in the mirror. She loved the way the dress draped over her curves—which weren't even all that curvy. For once in her life she felt both beautiful and powerful. "You've done too much already."

"That's where you're wrong." He walked toward her and took her hand. He lifted it to his lips and gently turned it over, and kissed her palm—an echo of how he'd kissed her months ago at the coronation. Her palm sizzled, and awareness reverberated in her belly, her nipples, even down to her toes, which were bare on the stone floor. "I'm just getting started."

He took one more step forward, pulled her into his arms and kissed her full and hard on the lips.

7

Lorenzo had been craving the taste of Beatriz for days. Kissing her was a risk. She was wary of men— of him—and rightfully so. He knew that if he moved in too fast he'd scare her off. He'd vowed to take his time and win her trust before doing anything that might send her guard shooting up.

But he couldn't resist.

She looked so breathtaking in the silver-gray dress she'd designed. The way the fabric draped over her body—which was usually hidden behind dark, formless attire—he wanted to run his fingers over those curves and hollows and get between the fabric and her skin.

And she was kissing him back. Arousal snapped through him as he felt her hands on his back, fingertips digging into his shirt.

Beatriz Leone was turning out to be full of surprises. He'd expected her to be prim and proper— which she was. He'd known she was tightly bound to her family and the confines of the palace. He'd wondered how he'd get past her reserve and win her over enough to become intimate.

He hadn't expected a woman with a rich creative imagination and a secret passion she'd never dared to explore.

Of course right now the passion was for fashion, not him. He wasn't kidding himself about that. He wasn't part of her circle. If anything he was the dangerous rake in those dusty novels she read in the palace library.

But she'd come out of her shell enough to show him her drawing and to see it come to life in silk. And right now he was running his hands over her creation and feeling the warm, exciting and unexpected woman beneath.

He deepened the kiss, daring to slip his tongue between her teeth and enjoy the electric thrill of touching hers. He allowed his eager hand to move lower and gently cup her delicious rear, so temptingly displayed in her cleverly cut dress.

He was just wondering if he dared to slide his other hand up to her breast when he heard a low moan escape his throat.

Lorenzo cursed the sound, especially since it made Beatriz stiffen and pull back. Now he'd overdone it. He opened his eyes to see her staring at him, blinking with surprise. Then she lifted a hand to her mouth and wiped it.

He racked his brain for the right thing to say, but for once he came up short. Beatriz wasn't the kind of easy party girl he could sling a well-worn line at.

She was aroused too. He could see her nipples tight underneath the fine silk. Her chest rose and fell faster than it should. Even if she hadn't expected his kiss, she'd enjoyed it.

"I wasn't planning to kiss you." That was the best he could come up with.

"Oh." A tiny crease appeared between her dark

brows. Was she wondering if he regretted it?

"I just wanted to see the dress, but I got carried away."

"I guess I should take it off." Suddenly she was awkward and shy.

"No, not yet." If she took it off now and disappeared he might never get close to her again. "Let me take some pictures of you in it."

"What for?"

"For you. You could send them to your sister." She'd mentioned going to fashion week with one of them.

She bit her lip—which sent heat rocketing to his groin—and he could see he'd caught her attention. "That's not a bad idea. Let me get my phone." She turned and walked over to where she'd left her bag and clothes.

He watched her from behind with a silent sigh. He'd give a fairly large sum of money to slide his arms around her and start up where they'd left off right now.

Patience, Lorenzo. He'd learned early on that in real estate deals and romance, it didn't pay to rush things.

She bent over—*be still my beating heart*—and retrieved her phone from her bag. "Let me set it up."

He loved the way the dress draped over her hips as she walked back. The seams were in just the right places to emphasize the subtle lines of her body. Lines he'd like to explore with his tongue...

"Here, all you have to do is press the camera icon." She handed it to him with a nervous frown, then went and stood awkwardly in front of him.

"Hmm, we need to set it up better. Perhaps you should stand in front of the mirror so I can capture the front and back at the same time."

She turned to look and saw both of their reflections in the mirror. "But won't you be in the picture then?"

"I suppose I would."

"And I don't really want anyone to know I was here. Why would I be at the Orangerie? It was Dad's retreat. It would seem strange. Let's find something neutral for me to stand against."

They walked through two medium-sized rooms, one a library and the next a dining room, and settled on a plain white wall in the hallway beyond. He lifted the camera to his eyes and pressed, then checked the image. "Too dark. There isn't enough light in here. Is there another room with white walls?"

She pressed a finger to her mouth, thinking. "One of the bedrooms is white."

Bedroom? His excitement ratcheted higher. "Okay." He managed to sound cool and noncommittal.

She peered in through one door. "Wallpaper, too distinctive." Then another. "More wallpaper." When she tried the third door she walked in. "This will work."

He followed her into a bright white bedroom with a mahogany sleigh bed against one wall. Portraits of two eighteenth-century ancestors, pretty young girls, adorned the fireplace wall, but another wall was bare and white and had light shining on it from two windows opposite.

Beatriz positioned herself against it and he took a picture. "Perfect, now move and let me get some different angles."

She made as if to turn, then thought better of it. "I

feel silly. I'm sure what you have is fine."

"No, you need to show your sister how it falls when you move. Lift up your arm. Like this." He moved forward and picked up her right arm by the wrist and held it above her head. The movement drew him so close to her that her breast almost—almost—brushed his chest. The feel of her skin beneath his fingers stoked his desire to red heat. "Perfect, just hold it like that."

"I feel weird."

"You look amazing." He took a picture, then moved back to her and gently turned her to a three-quarter angle, with both hands in front of her, to reveal the lines of the back of the dress. "Don't move."

He took the picture, then went back to lift her arms over her head. As he raised them past his lips, impulse stopped him and he kissed her hands, then her mouth. Then her neck and her cheek and soon his mouth roamed over her shoulders, then kissed her breasts through the soft gown.

His brain fogged with desire, he wasn't thinking, just reacting to her warm response. Her fingers thrust into his hair, her nails raking down his back. She wanted him too, and that aroused him almost to the point of insanity.

Don't go too fast. He had a plan here, a vision, and he wanted to win Beatriz over gently.

But there was nothing gentle about the feelings raging in him right now. Beatriz's fingers plucked at the buttons of his shirt, and he felt her hands slide underneath it, cool against his hot skin.

He groaned, but this time she didn't stop. She kissed him back as hard as he was kissing her. Her chest heaved and bumped against his, driving him deeper into a feverish state of arousal.

"We need to take the dress off carefully," he managed. He didn't want it to get ruined and leave her with a bad feeling about this encounter.

"Oh." She looked surprised, like she'd forgotten it. Her dark eyes wide with passion, she fiddled with the zipper cleverly hidden at the waist. He helped her, and together they worked it gently off over her head. He placed it carefully on a chair, out of harm's way.

"Now, where was I?" He could hear his own voice gruff with raw need. The sight of Beatriz's beautiful braless breasts and modest white panties almost unhinged him. She wasn't the type to wear scanty lace lingerie—she was so different from any woman he'd ever met. Normally so restrained, right now Beatriz was on fire with desire—just like him.

He licked and sucked her lips and nipples, both pink with arousal. They tore off his clothes until his erection came free and bumped against her. Even then she didn't hesitate or pull back—it must be true what they said about those quiet librarian types.

He was kneeling on the floor, mouth roaming closer to the magical area between her legs when a horrible thought occurred to him.

"I don't have a condom," he rasped. "I didn't…I didn't think we'd—"

He heard her inhale. "Me neither. And I'm not on…anything."

Damn! The curse stayed silent, but it rang through his whole being. Then a wild thought occurred to him. "Do you think your dad might have any around somewhere?"

She laughed. Then frowned. "I suppose it can't

hurt to check. He had guests stay here from time to time."

He grabbed towels from the adjoining bathroom and together they set off to explore. He had a feeling that if any of her brothers caught him like this—naked, erect and looking for a condom to impale their sister—he'd be in for the fight of his life.

But they weren't here, and he was. Beatriz led them into her father's bedroom, a gloomy chamber decorated with dark paintings of dead pheasants and foxes and triumphant hounds. "We can check the bathroom."

She looked unbearably delicious in the simple white towel, with her long dark hair cascading down her back. "You have lovely hair."

Her hand flew to it. "Oh, it's just brown. I usually tie it up."

"I know. I feel privileged to see it in all its glory." To see her in all her glory. He knew that Beatriz was not one to sleep around.

She pulled open the medicine cabinet and there was an array of pill bottles and shaving equipment but no condoms. They looked in the bedside table, which was filled with random papers but again no condoms.

Beatriz bit her lip—a gesture that was starting to drive him near-mad with desire. "It was a long shot. I'm pretty sure my dad had a vasectomy because he had five sets of twins in about ten years, then no children since."

"Makes sense. Or you might be one of twenty."

"Or thirty," she giggled. He couldn't believe how relaxed she seemed given their awkward circumstances. "And I suppose guests bring their own protection and take it when they leave. I have a bad feeling that we're not going to find anything."

"Don't worry about it. Come with me." He'd show her how much he could give—without asking for anything in return.

He took her back into the white bedroom, climbed up on the bed and kissed and caressed her all over. He could tell she trusted him not to enter her—and that warmed his heart. He licked and sucked her sensitive tissues until her orgasm made her cry out with pleasure, legs shaking and stomach muscles shivering with tension.

He was ready to pull his trousers back on over his blue balls, but she swiftly batted his clothes aside and took him in her mouth. He could tell she didn't really know what she was doing—which endeared her to him all the more—but he was already aroused to the point of explosion and came within seconds. Mercifully he managed to aim into the towels they'd brought, making Beatriz laugh rather than gag.

Spent, he collapsed onto the bed, tugging her into his arms. "That was amazing, Beatriz. Truly wonderful."

"Unexpected." She gazed at him with her big dark eyes. "I liked it."

Her sweet, honest comment further unmanned him. "Me too."

He could hardly believe she wasn't trying to run away or hastily dress in her dour dark clothing. Instead she gently ran her fingers through his hair and stroked his stubbly cheek. "I mean it, Beatriz, about the collection—for next fall and winter. Take it as a challenge. Spring fashion week is your deadline, and I'll be there to help you every step of the way."

He did mean it. He had no idea where this whole

thing was going, or if he'd ever get to develop that lake the way he'd dreamed of, but damn he wanted to see Beatriz shine, and turn to face her family with a smile, proving to them that she wasn't just the quiet one that no one noticed or remembered.

"It sounds crazy," she murmured, toying with the bedding. "Like an impossible dream that couldn't ever really come true." Her long lashes flicked up as she gazed at him. "I know I couldn't do it by myself. I'd lose confidence."

"That's why I'm here." He rubbed her back. "Execution is my strength. What I lack in creativity I make up for in my ability to get the job done."

He could count on one hand the times he'd failed to achieve his objective—and those were only because he hadn't achieved them…yet.

"All right." She inhaled, and he felt her breasts rise against his chest. "I'll do my best. I'll put together some drawings, and hopefully by next week they'll be ready to take to samples. This time I'm paying for it, though."

"Fine by me." He wanted this project—this dream—to be hers, and he knew she had the money. "I'll look into renting the venue for the show. I don't think we can start too early on that, and it will give you something concrete to envisage.

She swallowed and he could tell she was nervous. "What if it's a huge flop?"

"It won't be."

"How can you be so sure?" She looked up at him with those wide brown eyes.

"Business savvy." He managed a sly grin. "Trust me. I know what I'm doing."

She blew out a slow breath. "I'll try to embrace

your confidence."

"Perfect." He embraced her body, drawing her close, breathing into her beautiful hair and inhaling her sweet scent. "But right now I think we need to get you back to the palace."

"Oh, no. You can't drive me there."

"I not only can drive you there, but I absolutely intend to do it."

8

Beatriz was still in a state of disembodied bliss as she showered with Lorenzo in the big marble double shower. She couldn't believe they'd had sex—yet without having sex. It was so sweet and thoughtful of Lorenzo to pleasure her when they didn't have a condom, and she was so glad she'd been able to do the same for him.

He'd given her so much when he had her drawing made into a dress, how could she ever repay him? And he seemed to genuinely enjoy her company, her ideas, her dreams.… It was all too wonderful, and she kept feeling like she was about to wake up.

Which she was, if he took her back to the palace.

They toweled off and dressed in their crumpled clothes. "You really can't drive me home. They're way too nosy. And my Aunt Liesel is in town. She's the biggest gossip in Europe."

"She won't recognize me."

"She'd recognize anyone whose face has ever been on a social page in one of her magazines. Perhaps you can drop me off in the village and I'll call for someone to pick me up."

"You could have someone pick you up here."

Beatriz frowned. "No. I don't want anyone to

know I was here. Especially since we've made two towels wet and rumpled the bedding!" She hurried to smooth out the elaborate bedspread.

Lorenzo hung the towels back in the bathroom. They really should dry up all the drops of water scattered everywhere, but it wasn't a murder scene. They'd dry by themselves as long as no one came over there today.

"There's no way I'm letting you walk back after those sinister texts you were sent."

He had a point. Given the alarming events going on lately, she shouldn't be walking about unattended. Which made it awfully difficult to carry on a clandestine affair. "Maybe you could drop me right at the gate. Then I can walk up the drive under the full view of the guards." The guards at the gate wouldn't know Lorenzo from anyone else.

"Deal."

They drove slowly through town, and Beatriz found herself wondering if anyone glancing her way would be able to see how she'd spent her afternoon. As they pulled onto the road toward the palace she started to get nervous. "You won't kiss me at the gate."

"Is that an order?" He turned to her with a raised eyebrow.

"I think so." She felt sheepish about how her anxiety had come out, but for someone to see them kissing would be a disaster. "I don't want anyone to start asking questions."

"I understand." He looked straight ahead. "I'll be the very soul of discretion."

They approached the big gates at the end of the drive, where two guards always sat in the guard house.

As Lorenzo drew close to the closed gate he started to roll the window down. "Don't roll it down!" she gasped. "I don't want them to talk to you."

"Goodness. Anyone would think I was a wanted criminal." She saw a smile tug at his mouth.

"They're so nosy—the guards—it's their job." Beatriz immediately unbuckled her seat belt and got ready to leap out with a curt goodbye.

But the guards approached the car and tapped on Lorenzo's window. She leaped out and was about to slam the door and walk through the pedestrian gate when one guard said, "Princess Beatriz! I didn't realize it was you. Please drive on." And the big gates started to open.

"Oh, no. It's okay. I can walk from here."

"That's not necessary," said the guard. "Do drive."

Rather than make a scene she got back in the car, panic spiking through her. "Drive," she whispered.

Lorenzo, who appeared to be fighting a smile, drove.

"I'm sorry to be so rude." She realized how she must sound. "But this kind of thing makes me so nervous."

"It's okay, I understand." He didn't look rattled. "It's not easy being a princess with a large entourage snooping on you everywhere you go."

"Tell me about it." She peered ahead as they drove down the long, tree-lined drive. As soon as they got to the courtyard, she leaped out. "I had a wonderful time," she whispered. "And thanks for the dress." She held the precious black bag in her hand."

"You're more than welcome. I'll call you."

She didn't hang around for more pleasantries—or for anyone in the family to spot his car from the window—but struck out for the front steps, clutching her bag and trying to make up a story about where it was from.

The front door opened before she got there to reveal Darias looking uncharacteristically agitated. "Beatriz! My God, we've been worried sick. Where were you? Mom was calling you two hours ago, and we couldn't find you. We called the castle to see if you'd gone there, but they said you never showed up. The groom said he saw you walking out the side gate into the woods. We've had guards combing the woods."

"I'm fine, as you can see." She steeled herself. "I just went shopping."

"Who was that in the Audi?"

"Just a friend." She could never think on her feet in these situations. "I bought a dress."

Ack. She hated herself for lying, but she'd rather die than explain the whole situation, especially since things had gotten so out of hand with Lorenzo. Her body still throbbed and pulsed in places she'd almost forgotten existed. All she wanted to do was run to her room and collapse.

"Thank goodness you're okay, sweetheart." Her mom appeared behind him. "I can't believe you went out without an escort after Gibran warned us not to."

"I'm fine." Now was not the time to mention the strange texts. "I'm tired. Is it okay if I go to my room or do I need an armed guard to accompany me?"

Darias laughed. "Sorry, sis. You just had us freaked again. Are you living a double life?"

"If I was trying to I wouldn't get very far with you guys on my case." She managed a shaky smile. She walked past them and headed for the stairs, clutching the bag with her dress.

"You were out in a blue Audi the other day when Anna the cook saw you in town."

She kept walking.

"Who were you with?"

"No one important." With that she turned into the upstairs hallway and rushed for her door. Right now she was mad at Lorenzo for insisting on driving her home. She'd almost rather be accosted by an unknown assailant than be interrogated by all her family members at once—and if history was any guide, they wouldn't stop until they figured out who was driving the car.

I have to tell security about the texts. Beatriz had hung the dress in the back of her closet, showered again— this time washing her hair, which had still smelled tauntingly of Lorenzo—and battened on her usual bland expression. But now her heart was pounding.

How much did she have to tell them?

She walked into the living room, where her mom sat with Emma and Serena, while Serena's cute little dog Lucky sniffed at the antique rug. "Um, any idea where I can find Gibran?"

Her mom's eyes widened. "Gibran? Why? What's wrong?"

Beatriz struggled to keep her expression neutral. "Nothing really. I just wanted to ask him a question."

"I have his number programmed into my phone. Here." Emma thrust her phone out.

Beatriz copied the number into her phone, wondering why she hadn't put it there already. "Thanks."

She made to leave the room so she could call him.

She didn't want to scare her mom.

"Don't go too far, love. Dinner will be ready any moment."

"I won't." She went into a little-used pool room and closed the door, then she dialed Gibran's number. "Hi, it's Beatriz. I'm sure it's no big deal, but I thought I should tell you about some texts I got earlier." She explained the situation, saying that she'd left the stables for a walk in the woods—implying that she was on her horse but not actually stating it.

"I need to see your phone. I'll meet you in the pool room."

Beatriz's blood ran cold. How did Gibran know where she was right now? "Uh, okay."

She deleted the entire thread of messages from Lorenzo in her phone—which made her a little sad—and also edited her logged calls to remove any calls from him. Then she pulled up the strange texts. A knock on the door made her jump, which didn't make any sense but she was so wound up.

"Let me see." Gibran was so gruff and straightforward, unlike everyone else she'd met. Someone had told her he was the illegitimate son of a king in his homeland, which was actually worse than being the older female twin who wouldn't inherit. She'd probably like him if she wasn't so scared of him.

She thrust her phone forward. Gibran squinted at the short exchange. "Me too? Why would he start with that. What was he replying to?"

Beatriz opened her mouth. Then closed it. She'd typed, "I'm here," to Lorenzo, but now that whole thread was gone. If she told him that he'd know she was hiding something. Now she wished she hadn't deleted the Lorenzo thread. "I think he was able to read another text I sent to someone else."

"Where's that?"

She swallowed and felt a pulse start to pound in her temple. Why did she have to be so secretive about Lorenzo? For once in her life she'd met someone who really seemed to care about her. Someone who wanted to listen to her ideas. Someone who even found her attractive. It wasn't fair that her family was prejudiced against him.

But she wasn't going to lie. "I deleted it."

"Why?" His expression didn't change.

She chewed her lip. "It was to someone my brother Darias doesn't like. A man. I met with him yesterday."

"Why doesn't Darias like him?" Again, stone-faced.

"He's from an old rival family. Some nonsense that goes back for centuries. Honestly, I don't get it. If Darias finds out he'll think he's trying to use me or hurt me."

"Hmmph." Gibran grunted. "Mind if I pull that thread back up?"

"Once it's deleted? You can do that?"

"Yes." He didn't even look at her.

"Okay." Her voice was a shaky whisper. She watched, silent and almost tearful as Gibran managed to resurrect her thread of messages with Lorenzo.

"What's this about a dress?"

"I designed one, and he helped me get it made." She squeezed the words out reluctantly.

Gibran stared at her. "That's it? Why the secrecy? Why would you delete the messages?"

She shrugged. "I don't want the rest of the family

to know about the dress. They'll laugh at me. My dad hated the idea of me designing clothes." She attempted to appeal to his royal-outsider side. "When you're royal people have all kinds of stupid ideas about who you should and shouldn't be. It's nothing important, really."

Gibran's gaze remained steady. Then "hmmph" again. He handed her phone back. "I have no need to tell anyone about the dress, but I don't advise keeping any relationships a secret right now. There's too much at stake. And you really mustn't leave the palace without an escort. I've assigned Nina Hagen to protect you at all times."

"I know."

"So why didn't you alert her that you were leaving?"

Beatriz swallowed. "I guess I forgot."

"We think there are elements within the palace working against the family, so be on your guard."

"I will. Do you mean staff members?"

"I do. We're interviewing them, but most have been here for years and it's very hard to identify anyone suspicious."

"You think a staff member could have dug up the bodies and cut off—" She couldn't even say it.

"We do. Come to me immediately if you have any suspicions, no matter how small. Did anyone see you leaving the stables?"

"Matteo was around somewhere. He usually is. He's the only groom left in the stables. He's been with the palace for years, maybe his entire working life." This was true of many staffers. Palace jobs were the most prized employment in Altaleone because they paid well and came with a handsome pension.

She had no idea how old Matteo was, maybe late thirties or early forties? He wasn't chatty, at least not with her. He was more of a man's man.

"I'll look into him more closely."

"I'm sure he wasn't involved. He was very close to my father." She shuddered at the idea that anyone close to them could be considered a real suspect. But at least Gibran wasn't asking probing questions about her and Lorenzo. No one needed to know they'd made love.

A hot memory of their time together assaulted her and she felt heat rise up her neck. "Can I go back to the living room? If I'm late for dinner my mom will worry."

"Of course." He held her gaze, then his eyes narrowed. "Next time you need to meet with Lorenzo be sure Nina is with you."

She gulped. "Okay." So he suspected something, even if no one else did.

"Someone is trying to scare you. To put you on edge. You should be wary—we've had two murders and Emma was kidnapped so we don't know what to expect. As the reigning king's twin sister you should consider yourself at high risk of foul play."

"I know." She moved for the door, desperate to get away from him. "I appreciate your discretion."

He made another grunting sound—no royal charm for Gibran—and she exited into the hallway. The family was heading into dinner, and she hurried to join them, heart still thudding like a runaway train.

It was pretty sad when you were more scared of your family's opinion than you were of an unknown weirdo who'd somehow gained access to your phone.

"Beatriz!" Darias called to her from across the

dining room. The urgent tone in his voice startled her and she almost tripped on the edge of the ancient carpet. "What's going on?" He strode toward her. "Why were you out with Lorenzo Aldobrando?"

9

Beatriz' heart sank. *I snuck out through the woods to meet him, then we went to Dad's old hideaway to have steamy sex.* "He took me out to lunch."

She could almost feel her nose growing.

"Why?" Darias towered over her.

She kept going to the table and sat down, careful to keep her expression neutral. "Why not?" She took a fresh, hot roll from the basket.

"Are you serious? He's Lorenzo fricken Aldobrando. He's trying to get something out of you."

"Darias!" Emma cut in. "You don't know that." Beatriz wished she could reach across the table and hug her sister-in-law.

"You bet I do. His whole family are like that. They remind me of the Medicis."

"Then shouldn't one of them be pope?" asked Aunt Liesel with an arch expression.

"I'm sure they're working on it, but Lorenzo has obviously managed to avoid that duty, at least based on what I've heard about his fondness for the ladies." Darias took a swig of wine.

Beatriz felt herself shrinking. She managed to tear her roll and dip a corner of it in her tomato and bacon soup. "He didn't try to get anything out of me. He was very nice."

"All part of his dastardly plan, I'll bet." Darias frowned. "Did I tell you he tried—twice—to convince me to lease him the lake and the land around it? And I'm sure the lease was just a way of getting his claws into it so he could take ownership by fair means or foul."

"Oh, Darias, don't be so dramatic." Their mom shook out her napkin before putting it on her lap. "That land has been sitting unused for ages. There's nothing wrong with him asking to lease it."

"Dad told me from day one that the most important part of my duty as king was to maintain the territorial integrity of Altaleone."

"That's more important than taking care of its people?" Beatriz seized this opportunity to change the subject.

"Yes. People only live a short time, he said, and the land is what makes Altaleone a nation that continues from one century to the next."

"I suppose I can see his point," said Sandro. "But that seems a bit reactionary."

"A monarchy is reactionary," said Darias with a wry grin. "Continuity of tradition is the whole point. Of course I want to do everything I can to make life good for our people, but I don't intend to lose one square inch of the kingdom that was handed down to me."

"Life is already good for our people." Their mom helped herself to the salad that a staffer was taking around. "We have the highest per capita income and longest life expectancy on earth. I don't think there's a more robust measure of happiness than that."

Beatriz wasn't so sure. Still, she wasn't going to argue that Altaleone wasn't the best place on earth. She'd certainly never thought of living anywhere else.

"So the most important part of my job," Darias continued, uncharacteristically loud, "is to make sure that no one, including Lorenzo Aldobrando, manages to buy, sneak or steal our land out from under us."

"I hardly think he could do that even if he wanted to," murmured Beatriz, avoiding his intense gaze.

"Don't be so sure. His family has never ceased protesting and making a claim for that land. Every now and then some thousand-year-old agreement holds up in court somewhere in Europe. I don't intend for that to happen. If he wants it badly enough he might even try to marry you to get it."

Beatriz managed a fake laugh. It didn't sound very convincing. "Trust me, there was no marriage proposal. We simply shared an enjoyable conversation." *And some very pleasurable lovemaking.* She distracted herself from the memories with a sip of iced water.

"The whole thing sets my teeth on edge," said Darias. "And why did you go out without an armed escort?"

Beatriz felt her dander rising. "Darias, you may be king, but I'm still your sister, not your child." She hated talking like this in front of Sandro's new girlfriend, Serena, who probably felt awkward witnessing this family spat.

"He's only concerned about your safety, my love," said her mom. "I am too. Anything could have happened. You know Emma was kidnapped."

"I know. I won't do it again. It's not easy getting used to living like we're at war or something." She felt bad for worrying her mom. She had enough to deal with after losing Dad. "But don't be so neurotic. Lorenzo has just been friendly. He insisted on dropping me home so it's not like he was trying to hide from you. I bet he thought it was rude of me not to ask him in, but I know how you all feel about him and his family. Anyway, I'm more uptight and suspicious than all of you put together, so I can't believe you think I'd just fall into some trap."

"You have a point," said Sandro. "Still, Lorenzo is known as kind of a shark in the business world, so do be careful."

"A young lady in your position must always be careful," said Aunt Liesel, through a mouthful of bread roll. "When you have both money and a title you can never be sure which one they want more."

Unfortunately Beatriz had to agree with her. She'd learned early on that being a princess was a major liability when it came to dating. Now that her grandmother had left her a large personal inheritance, she was even more of a catch for some unscrupulous male.

"Why don't you ask him to come over for dinner?" asked her mom. "So we can get to know him better?" Her usual warm expression didn't hide an edge of genuine curiosity in her voice.

"Sure. I'll ask him next time I talk to him. Not that it will be any time soon. Like I said, we're just friends." She had no intention of doing any such thing. After Darias's performance tonight she could just imagine how he'd rake Lorenzo over the coals and possibly—she almost died just having the thought—accuse him to his face of trying to marry Beatriz for her inheritance.

"What did the two of you talk about?" Sandro looked up from his glass of wine. "I'm just curious."

We were planning my ascent to the pantheon of European fashion designers. "Oh, this and that." Could she tell them about the dress without going into too much detail about her big dreams? She doubted they'd remember she'd wanted to be a designer. It hadn't come up for years. "He likes to ride. You know I could talk about horses all day."

"That is true," teased Sandro. "If he's a rider he's perfect for you."

"Don't encourage her," said Darias with a glare. "I can see why traditionally monarchs liked to arrange marriages for all their sisters and daughters. That's very tempting right now."

"Throwing a bread roll at you is very tempting right now." Beatriz lifted a brow. "I thought you considered yourself a feminist. Becoming king seems to be having a devastating effect on your respect for human rights."

"Ouch." Darias made a wry expression. "I guess you're right. It's weird…suddenly I feel responsible for everyone in a way I never did before. I must be driving Emma crazy with it too."

"Only a little." Emma smiled. Emma was quite possibly the nicest person on earth—well, maybe after their mom. Nothing ever made either of them mad enough to yell at someone. They were both the kind of warm, giving women men dreamed of marrying—unlike her, the prickly, awkward one who was suspicious of everyone and usually said the wrong thing.

A flashback to her afternoon in Lorenzo's arms almost stole her breath. She didn't feel awkward when she was with him. He was easygoing and encouraging, and he made her relax and reveal things she'd vowed never to tell anyone, hopes and dreams she'd almost forgotten she had. And the way he kissed...

"...can you promise me that?" Darias had asked her a question. She hadn't heard it.

"What?"

"Earth to Beatriz," chimed in Sandro with a cheeky grin.

"I was just thinking about something." Like Lorenzo's hard, flat stomach.

"I can see that." Darias's eyebrow lifted. "I just want you to promise to always take a security escort with you when you leave the palace."

"Yes, your majesty."

"Beatriz!" their mom protested. "He's just concerned about your safety. We all are."

"I know. I'm just bitter that he gets to be king even though I was born first." It was better to openly joke about it than to fester over it. "Would that happen in America, Serena?"

Sandro's girlfriend looked startled. Then she shrugged. "I wish I could say it wouldn't, but I suppose we'd need to elect a woman president to prove that Americans are comfortable with a female leader."

"True." Beatriz lifted her glass. "We women have our work cut out for us."

"Come on, Beatriz. You don't even have a job." Sandro cocked his head. "You haven't ever had one."

"Nor have you, bro. Didn't you try that once and you got fired on the second day?"

"They simply asked me to offer my resignation." His eyes sparkled with mischief. Nothing rattled

Sandro. She envied his cool. "Besides, I run my own business."

"Maybe I should start a business." She blinked. They had no idea she was already planning it.

"You don't have to do that, sweetheart," protested her mom. "You fulfill a very important role here."

"Opening school buildings and giving out companies' year-end awards."

"A woman's work is more subtle but every bit as important," said Liesel smugly. As far as Beatriz knew Liesel had never worked a day in her life. Her existence revolved around riding her horse and driving people nuts. More things they had in common... "One doesn't want to lower oneself."

Beatriz fought the urge to roll her eyes. "There seems to be a very short list of acceptable professions for princes and princesses."

"That's why I ignored it and became an artist anyway," said Darias with a wink. Their soup bowls were cleared away and replaced with plates of glazed salmon and green beans. "I'm still painting too. I told my gallery I'd be ready for a new show by the end of the year."

How did Darias get away with doing something "frivolous"? That was the word her dad had used to describe her fashion school dream. Because Darias didn't ask anyone's permission and just did it.

As his older sister, she intended to take a page from his book. Hopefully they would learn of her new venture when she showed them glowing articles in the press. She had to work to keep a smile off her face at the prospect.

"I think it's wonderful that you're still painting, sweetheart," said their mom.

"Emma encouraged me." Darias leaned over and gave Emma a tender kiss. "And how could I not paint with inspiration this lovely beside me every day? It would be torture."

"Your paintings should command a higher price now that you're king," said Liesel sharply. "If they don't, then fire your gallery."

Darias laughed. "I have no say in the pricing. It's what the market commands, according to Keane Moss, my gallery owner. And I trust him. He hired Emma. We'd never have met if it wasn't for him."

"And me," cut in Sandro. "I suggested you marry her, remember?"

"Yep. Before I'd even said a single word to her."

"What can I say, I have a good eye." He turned and smiled at Serena—who looked alarmed, then slowly smiled back. Beatriz wondered if Serena would turn out to be "the one" for Sandro. She didn't remember him ever looking at another woman like that.

If Sandro and Darias—two unrepentant playboys—could find love, then why was it so wrong for her to have a relationship with Lorenzo?

It wasn't. And, like her fashion line, she was going to pursue her relationship with him using as much discretion—or even secrecy—as she could manage.

Beatriz didn't want anyone, even the staff, to see her drawing, so she did most of it at night after everyone had headed for their separate rooms. She visited the old art supply shop in the village to stock up on paper, pens and watercolors, taking Gibran's female security guard with her, but no one seemed to notice or care. Sketching and painting were perfectly acceptable princessly activities, after all.

Lorenzo called her, and they chatted about horses and cities they liked and how he'd like to kiss her all over. "It's entirely possible that someone, possibly even the palace security, is listening in on this phone call."

"We're not discussing anything criminal."

"True, but you should have heard the reaction when I told them I met with you. You'd think I'd handed over the keys to the kingdom."

"When can I see you again?"

She smiled. He wasn't easily deterred. "I don't know. We should lay low for a while."

"Tomorrow sounds good. I'll come pick you up at ten."

"What? No! You can't come here. Besides, I ride my horse at ten."

"Then ride your horse at eight. I need to come early so we have time to drive to Milan. I want to show you two possible venues for your show."

"Already? I can't believe you even started looking into that."

"Fashion week is very busy. The best venues are booked years in advance."

Beatriz chewed her lip. "I can meet you in town, but I have to bring a security guard. She'll drive in a car behind me." So much for any romantic kissing.

"That's fine. The usual street at ten?"

"Okay."

"Sleep well, beautiful. I hope your dreams are all about me."

"You would," she teased, but she couldn't stop smiling. "You sleep well too."

Beatriz ended the call, wondering how her telling

him she wanted to lay low translated into him meeting her tomorrow. He made her smile. Truth be told, his persistence and refusal to take no for an answer were the reasons he'd managed to get this close to her. She had decades of experience with keeping everyone at arm's length.

And she couldn't wait to see Lorenzo again.

Cunning as he reputedly was, she had a feeling he'd figure out a way for them to be alone and away from the security guard for at least a few stolen moments. And she couldn't wait…

10

The drive to Milan went smoothly, considering the subfreezing temperatures and banks of snow piled high on either side of the roads out of mountainous Altaleone. Even as they descended the mountain passes, Lorenzo's hands strayed to touch her and his stolen glances and sexy half-smiles underscored the attraction between them. They arrived in the city almost forty-five minutes before their first appointment and stopped at a café.

Beatriz had a notebook of sketches in her bag—nothing final—to show to Lorenzo. Half of her wondered if he'd take one look at them and change his mind about this whole crazy idea of her having a show at fashion week. After they'd ordered, she pulled it out with trembling fingers.

"They're just ideas," she muttered. "I don't really have a theme, and I should." He looked through the sketches, pausing to consider each one. Her pulse ratcheted up as she watched his serious expression. Was he trying to figure out how to offer critique without crushing her?

He handed the notebook back. "I can't wait to see them." His eyes glowed with pleasure. "They're beautiful."

Her chest filled with emotion. His fingers brushed hers as she took the book and stirred her senses, too. "I was thinking that perhaps Signora Pazzi could come with me to choose some of the fabrics. She'll know what will be easy to sew into a certain design— and I'm sure she has connections at the best fabric showrooms in Milan. I could pay her a consulting fee."

"Sounds like you've got it all figured out, and all I need to do is sit back and admire your collection." He raised his coffee cup. "Soon you'll be the toast of the town."

Beatriz sipped her coffee—it was strong and slightly spicy. She could just imagine the looks on her family's faces when she told them she was having a show. Or maybe she shouldn't tell them until afterward? It would be embarrassing if they came, and it bombed and everyone in the audience whistled and jeered. Could that even happen at a fashion show?

"What's wrong?" asked Lorenzo.

Her anxiety must be showing on her face. "What if it's a disaster?"

He laughed, then took her hands and squeezed them, as if to reassure her with his firm, warm grip. "How can it be? It's going to be a smashing success."

Most of the usual venues were long rented by established designers, but Lorenzo's contacts had found a couple of options. The first venue was an elegant old mansion with a double-roomed ballroom that could accommodate a runway. It also had a pretty formal garden that would be perfect for a reception afterward. Beatriz could almost hear champagne glasses clinking and people whispering her name in shocked awe.

The second venue was an old armory that had been renovated into a modern art gallery space. It was more dramatic and somehow more professional than the first, but the room was so large she worried that it would be hard to fill. She felt very small in it and worried that her collection would too.

"I like the first one," she said, as they exited onto the street. "It's not as hip-looking, but I think it will be a better backdrop for my clothes. Let's face it, my designs all have a traditional aspect to them."

"I liked it better too. More intimate. And I do love a beautiful old building that retains all its original features."

"Me too!" she exclaimed. Then she giggled. "Maybe it's because we're both from such ancient families, we can't help it." She and Lorenzo did have a lot in common. His family wasn't technically royalty, but they'd been large landowners for as long as her family, if not longer. Besides, she was pretty sure his family's land had been a principality at some point before Italy was unified, so he probably was royalty if you went back far enough.

Not that it mattered to her. It was just nice not to have to worry about him thinking her too Old World or too rich or snobby. She was always anxious about being judged because she was a princess, but she never felt like Lorenzo was judging her.

"I can't wait to see what you do with the lake house."

His words startled her so much that she almost tripped on the pavement.

"Uh." She'd almost forgotten that she told him she

had plans for it. "I haven't gotten started on it yet. My family does use it from time to time. My brother Sandro has something going on there tomorrow." Some ridiculous secret society initiation. She couldn't believe he'd even consider joining the Cross of Blood when the cultish organization seemed to be linked to their father's and grandmother's deaths. Possibly it was part of their attempt to learn more about it—maybe even to infiltrate it and look for clues to the murders—but no one ever told her anything.

"You don't mind?"

I don't really have a choice. Darias had casually asked her—this morning—if they could meet there. He'd have been shocked if she'd said no. She didn't want Lorenzo to know that no one really cared if she minded or not. She shrugged and tried to sound nonchalant. "No. It's just sitting empty."

"Have you thought of moving there yourself?"

"As a residence?" Her eyes widened. "I don't need one. There's plenty of room at the palace."

He opened the door of the car for her. She felt conscious of the security guard's gaze on her from the car parked across the street. Lorenzo walked around to the driver's side. "But don't you ever want some privacy? A space of your own? Somewhere to decorate to your own taste?"

She chewed her lip. "I hadn't really thought about it." She always assumed she'd move out when she finally got married—an event she'd all but given up thinking about. She certainly wasn't going to tell Lorenzo that, though. "Living at the palace is convenient because the stables are there and the indoor arena is really the only way I can ride in winter. Of course my dad isn't there to ride with, but my mom really needs me because otherwise she'd get lonely and…" She realized she was rambling and that Lorenzo was just staring at her.

"You're so beautiful." He fixed that slate-gray, heart-melting gaze on her. "May I kiss you?"

He must be asking because of the guard. In a way she didn't mind the guard seeing. Everyone at the palace probably thought of her as Boring Beatriz, who'd never scandalize her loving family by kissing the scion of their ancient enemy.

How ridiculous that was! As if a grudge could really continue from generation to generation. "I'd love that."

He leaned in and his lips met hers in a hot welcome.

Beatriz felt herself melt into his arms. Since they'd made love she'd thought about little else than being in his arms again. He'd made her feel so alive, sexy, beautiful—things she'd never truly felt before. "I wish we weren't in the car," she whispered when their lips parted.

"I have a tiny pied-à-terre in Milan." He looked at her, a question in his eyes. "We could go there."

"I do need to be home for dinner, or my family will worry." She hated how she sounded like a teenager with a curfew. She was a grown woman for crying out loud! Still, with everything that was going on, she didn't want to alarm them.

"It's only a few streets away. Your security guard can park outside. We'll be back at the palace by one hour after dusk." He sounded hopeful.

"Okay. Let me tell Nina." She called and said they were stopping into a building briefly and she could park nearby. "Let's go."

She felt a thrill of excitement as they pulled out of the parking space and headed through the streets. No one needed to know how she spent her afternoon, and Nina had promised total discretion. He used a remote to open a solid gate and drive into a cobbled courtyard, then closed the gate behind them.

A carved door led them to a flight of stone stairs and up into a beautiful apartment decorated with fine Milanese antiques set against pure white walls and delicate textiles. "It belonged to my aunt Greta. She used it for her shopping trips since her family estate was so far from town. She left it to me when she died because she knew how much I love Milan."

"Were you close to her?"

"She was like a mother to me. Her last words were for me to find the right woman to marry. I've felt her watching over me ever since."

Beatriz fought the urge to glance over her shoulder. His aunt Greta probably didn't intend for him to use her pied-à-terre as a love nest. "How would she feel about you being here with me?"

He paused, looking at her. "She'd be happy." He said it softly, thoughtfully.

Was she the woman his beloved aunt would have wanted him to marry? He'd said almost as much. The thought flattered—and alarmed—her. Was he really that serious? His expression said he was. Her heart swelled at the prospect that Lorenzo might really want a future with her.

He took her hand and led her into a bedroom, also in soft white and warm wood. There he kissed her until her knees started to give way. She clung to him tighter, not afraid to lean on him. It felt good to sink into his strength—and rest.

Then she kissed him back, exploring the contours of his face, enjoying the roughness of his afternoon stubble and the warm male smell of him.

She unbuttoned his shirt, baring his hard tan chest. He pulled her sweater off over her head, then played with the long, tousled hair that came loose from her bun and fell over her shoulders.

Now, when they kissed, her nipples poked his chest through her lacy bra, which made them tingle with arousal. She soon found herself fumbling with his belt, wanting more. This time he had condoms and soon they were naked on the bed, exploring each other's bodies while the tension inside them built almost to breaking point.

Lorenzo didn't make her self-conscious. She didn't feel clumsy and inexperienced, like she had in previous fumbling encounters with the opposite sex. Everything flowed so naturally between them, and she kissed and caressed him all over, enjoying the new and unfamiliar pleasure that shimmered inside her.

When they couldn't stand it any more, she sheathed him and he entered her, slowly and with exquisite tenderness. They moved together, to the percussion of their own heartbeats and increasingly labored breath, their movements growing faster and more intense as emotion rushed through her.

I know why they call it making love. She could feel—something—building and growing between them, as their bodies shared such intense pleasure. They stroked and grabbed each other, passion rising to boiling point inside them. Eventually her climax got the better of her and she heard herself cry out—a strange, faraway sound—and she clung to him while shockwaves of sensation rolled through her and his own climax ripped a groan from his throat.

Afterward they lay in each others arms under the soft covers, her heart brimming with affection for this man who'd dared to breach her family's forbidding castle walls and pursue her in a way most men would never dare.

"You should redecorate the lake house," he whispered, as her head lay on his chest.

"What?" For a moment she didn't even know what he was talking about.

"You could breathe new life into it. I believe houses have energy, a life of their own, and we need to nurture it just like we would a garden."

Beatriz lifted her head. Thoughts of the lake house scattered the happy, romantic thoughts she'd been lost in like a stiff breeze. "I don't know. It's kind of far away from everything, and the road isn't all that great, especially in winter."

"It's not more than twenty minutes from the palace, and you can improve the road. You have connections in high places." His eyes twinkled with mischief.

"True." She didn't really like this whole idea. She'd been so pleased that he hadn't mentioned the lake house. When he'd first started talking to her she'd suspected that she was merely a stepping-stone to his goal of owning it, and now that she'd given herself up to him and was lying naked in his arms, suddenly he was bringing it up again. "I'd only do it for myself, though. I've decided that I'd never sell it."

She looked hard at him, wanting to gauge his reaction.

His gaze didn't flicker. "Of course not. But you could live there. The lake is so beautiful, and the house itself is quite architecturally unusual."

Was it? She didn't even know. Her dad had thought it ugly, but it was just the old house out by the lake to her. When had Lorenzo even been there? Her gut instincts told her to push back. "I don't know. I think I have enough to do with getting this collection ready." Suddenly her suspicions were returning. Maybe the whole collection was just a ruse so he could get close to her and trick her into handing over the house?

She rose off his chest and sat up in bed. "We'd better get ready to leave."

"So soon." His too-handsome face looked genuinely sad. "I wish I could hold you in my arms for ever."

"I have responsibilities," she said stiffly. She wondered if she'd been too easy.

"You're right, and I admire you for being such a pillar of your family." He climbed out of bed. She was already dressing. "And I promise I'll have you back in plenty of time to shower and change for dinner."

"Thanks." She dressed, still feeling wary.

"It's great that you have so many sketches already. When do you think you'll have the final versions for Signora Pazzi?"

"In a couple of weeks, I hope. I'm going to give her a call this week to hopefully set up an appointment to look at fabrics. I don't want to finalize the designs until I have some idea of what I'm working with. Fabric makes such a difference to the way a piece falls."

"True. Will I be allowed to come along on this shopping expedition?" He looked so hopeful, like a little kid hoping to be taken to the pet store.

"If you like." She wanted to laugh. He seemed to be enjoying this as much as her, which was just too sweet.

He made the bed and smoothed the covers, and the way his hand lingered on the soft white bedspread made her think of his mom and his feelings for her, which tugged at her heart and made her want to hug him again.

Her upbringing had made her so paranoid about people wanting to use her. Quite the reverse, Lorenzo had offered a helping hand so she could fulfill a private dream. She'd never have dared to embark on something like this by herself.

On the drive back, doubts started to creep in through all the cracks in her psyche. And not just doubts about Lorenzo. "What if I'm kidding myself and I can't pull off a good collection?"

"I have total confidence in you." He shot her a winning smile. "And since you have no boss you can keep tweaking until everything is just the way you want it."

She mulled that over. "What if no one comes to the opening? I'm an unknown. Why would anyone care about my designs?"

Now he laughed. "You're a princess. People care about everything you do. They'll come just because they're curious, even the fashion press."

"But I thought I was going to use an assumed name to avoid people making assumptions about me." She hadn't really thought about how much more difficult that would make it to get attention.

"You could, but wouldn't you rather have people know it's really you?"

She bit her lip. "I suppose so." Having her name

on it tugged at all her insecurities. "But what if people don't take my designs seriously because I'm a princess? They'll think it's just an idle pastime."

"The designs will speak for themselves. Have some more confidence in your talent. Everyone has to start somewhere. We'll put together a press release the week before, just long enough so people have time to make plans to come to the show, but not so long that they'll have time to form opinions before they see your work."

Beatriz inhaled deeply. "You make everything sound so easy."

"There's no reason to complicate matters. Make a plan, execute it and have faith that it will go as intended."

"It's that last part that I'm having trouble with. I guess I'm not much of a mover and shaker."

"That's okay. I am, so I'll help with that part." He leaned in and kissed her cheek—while driving at seventy kilometers per hour on a winding road. "It'll be a big success. Trust me."

Trust me. Beatriz had learned never to really trust any man—and she'd been strongly cautioned never to trust Lorenzo Aldobrando. Still, this was her dream and she was going to do her very best to make it come true.

"And this time I'm going to escort you home. There's no reason for us to be sneaking behind your family's back."

Beatriz felt adrenaline zing through her. But really, why shouldn't he meet them? They could put all the nastiness behind them and maybe she'd start to feel like they were a real couple with a future. She drew in a shaky breath. "Okay."

11

Beatriz felt her pulse accelerate as they pulled up to the main gates of the palace. Being winter it was already dark and she could see more guards than usual milling about and cars in the driveway. "I wonder what's going on?" she murmured, as they drew close.

Lorenzo rolled down the window and smiled at the guard in the gatehouse. "I'm escorting Princess Beatriz home."

"I'm sorry, sir, but we have orders not to let anyone outside the family into the palace."

"Why?" Beatriz felt panic rise in her chest. Had something happened?

"Just a precaution, your highness. There was an unwelcome visitor earlier today. Our security staff is on alert. Nina will drive you to the door."

She glanced at Lorenzo. "I'm sorry."

"No problem." He made an effort to look like he didn't mind, but she could tell he did.

"Another time." She unbuckled her seat belt. All this extra security was rattling her nerves. It was bad enough being followed everywhere by a virtual stranger. She wanted to kiss Lorenzo goodbye but restrained herself. She didn't need the staff gossiping.

"I'll call you later," he said softly before she closed

the door. She climbed into Nina's car and watched as the guards directed Lorenzo around a small loop and back out the gate.

"Nina, what's going on?"

Nina always looked thoroughly serious and professional, her hair tied back in a neat bun that sat tidily above the collar of her crisp shirt. "An American actress showed up to see Sandro and had to be escorted from the palace. Then there's an offsite event tonight and Gibran has called for full security. Every member of the household is under surveillance, including all the staff, and they're following everyone's movements closely."

Oh, yes, the Cross of Blood meeting. Her brother Sandro was being inducted. She rather wished she could go and see what all the fuss was about. It could hardly be dangerous with a phalanx of security guards hovering over the proceedings.

Nina drove her to the door, and she got out. Luckily no one was at the door to grill her about her whereabouts. In fact everyone seemed to be in rather a flap—even the staff were rushing about and tension crackled in the air.

She managed to change for dinner and get downstairs, fully prepared to describe her unsuccessful shopping trip to Milan, but no one seemed to care. Sandro and Serena were fussing over her little dog. Darias and Emma strode over and talked to them without even noticing her.

Only Aunt Liesel made a beeline for her. "Did you hear about it? She claims she's pregnant!"

Beatriz pretended to look like she cared. "Who?"

"Maya Dunham. The actress." She leaned in. "She insists that Sandro's the father."

"I had no idea they were involved." Beatriz regretted bringing Liesel here. She'd only done it to deflect attention from herself and Lorenzo. Now Liesel showed no signs of leaving and was likely to be even more nosy about Lorenzo than anyone else. Whoops.

"Oh, yes, it's been all over the papers, but I don't suppose you read them anyway."

"No, none of us do. It's important for staying sane." Not that she was ever mentioned.

"Well, you can imagine how that went over when Sandro is here with another woman." Liesel lifted a thin brow. "His new girlfriend was quite upset."

"I can imagine." But it was, in fact, hard to imagine. Serena was unbelievably cool and gracious, considering she'd been hurled headlong into the middle of the palace crisis. If anything Beatriz suspected the actress was lying. Sandro might love women, but he wasn't the type to two-time anyone and she could see he was besotted with Serena. And her little black-and-white dog, Lucky—who was adorable.

Beatriz would be madly jealous if it wasn't for Lorenzo looking at her in much the same way. She fought a smile that wanted to rush to her lips. Liesel was talking about her horse who had a suspensory ligament issue—again—and all she had to do was nod and look sympathetic. She tried not to think about how she might well end up like Liesel in twenty years, a bitter spinster rambling on about her horse's legs while people looked bored and nodded.

As they headed in to dinner it emerged that both Emma and Serena were going along to the Sandro's Cross of Blood initiation.

"But surely such a thing is unheard of," muttered Liesel. "The society is for titled aristocrats." She glared at Serena, who was not only American but African-American. Beatriz fought the urge to roll her eyes.

"If all goes according to plan, Serena will soon be a titled aristocrat," said Sandro, coolly, pulling out Serena's chair for her.

Beatriz stared. Had her brother just announced his intention to marry Serena? The whole table had fallen silent, no doubt as stunned as she was, so she decided to rush in and end the awkward lull. She turned to Serena. "I wish I could come to the Cross of Blood meeting. Do you know anything about the society?"

Serena, still staring at Sandro, didn't respond. Then she suddenly whipped her head around, worry in her eyes. "Sorry, what did you say?"

"Just that I'm envious. I've always been curious about the Cross of Blood. Grandmama was always very mysterious about it, and Papa always shushed me when I asked him about it." She turned to Darias, who'd just entered with Emma. "Can I come too?"

"Not this time," he replied. "With Serena and Emma attending we'll be quite a crowd. I don't want to unsettle them."

"Typical," said Beatriz with a pout. "You don't want me there because you don't trust me." Maybe they thought she'd share all their weird family secrets with Lorenzo. Not that he'd even be interested.

"Nonsense," said Darias. "There's just no reason for you to be there tonight."

Beatriz felt snubbed. She was his twin sister—his older sister—and Sandro's new girlfriend got to go? They weren't married yet. "What reason does Serena have to be there?" She stared at Darias, then at Sandro.

"Because she's my guest of honor." Sandro sipped his wine, nonchalant.

"I wish I could be somebody's guest of honor." She tried for a brave smile. "I am the oldest Leone here, after all. Perhaps I could be inducted into the society?"

Darias cocked his head. "You know it's just men."

"Grandmama was in it, wasn't she?"

"Only because she was queen, since there was no available male heir at the time her father died. According to Altaleone law that makes her an honorary man."

Beatriz laughed. You really couldn't win with this kind of nonsense. Besides, she'd rather be curled up in bed texting Lorenzo than standing around in a drafty, unheated ballroom. "Don't damage my house with any of your secret activities, okay?"

"Oh, come on, you never even go there," Darias challenged her. "When did you last even visit?"

She shrugged, suddenly deciding that she was definitely going to renovate the house and start using it. "It was a crime scene, and I didn't want to visit the scene of the deaths. But I'm planning to do something with the house soon. Grandmama would have wanted me to. She loved that house."

"She used it as a summer house for maybe five years in the 1970s," protested Lina. "Your father told me that she loved the summer breeze off the lake but used to complain about the weird sounds the house made. He always thought it was haunted."

Beatriz shivered. "Have fun there tonight, guys!" she teased. Still, she was going to head there tomorrow—with Lorenzo along for company just in case—to see what might be done with the place. She didn't like the idea that her brothers had spent more time there than she had. "Seriously though, stay safe."

"Gibran is bringing a task force. We'll be quite a convoy of cars. We're hoping to learn more about the members of this society and see if they're related to the murders."

"It all makes me very nervous," said her mom, putting her glass down with a shaky hand. "I rather wish you wouldn't do it."

"We can't live in fear, Mom," said Darias. He put his big hand over hers. "We're going to root the criminals out and make them pay."

Her mom glanced at Beatriz. "Well, Beatriz and I will be counting the moments until your safe return."

Suddenly Beatriz was glad she couldn't go. She knew her mom needed her, and she was happy to be there for her.

Back at home, Lorenzo poured himself a glass of wine and phoned his sister Steffi. Now it was just the two of them he made an effort to talk to her at least twice a week so they didn't drift apart like so many busy adult siblings.

"Hey, how'd it go with Signora Pazzi?" She'd hooked him up with the seamstress for Beatriz.

"Great. She was almost as quick as Cinderella's fairy godmother."

His sister chuckled. "And Beatriz was happy?"

"Thrilled. And she liked the experience so much that she's working on more designs. She's very talented."

"Talented, or beautiful?" Steffi saw him as a bit of

a playboy. And maybe he had been once, before he started burying himself alive in work.

"Both, Steff. Like you."

She laughed. "I bet you charmed her out of her clothes."

He inhaled slowly, remembering the deep pleasure they'd shared. "A gentleman doesn't kiss and tell."

"Even to his own sister? Come on. Am I allowed to tell people my brother is dating a princess?"

"No! Her family is very suspicious of me so we're keeping things under wraps for now. They think I'm just out to get my hands on her land."

"Are you?"

"Of course not."

Her silence spoke volumes. She cleared her throat. "Don't forget I know you better than you know yourself."

"Okay, I admit that striking lake property—abutting our own lovely mountainside—did spark my interest at first, but there's a lot more to Beatriz than her impressive holdings."

"And her sparkly tiara."

"She's blunt and funny and very creative." He smiled just thinking about her quirky expressions. "And surprisingly sweet. I really enjoy her company."

"I can hardly believe what I'm hearing. Then again, she is a princess. I suppose that could attract even the most hardened bachelor."

"Who says I'm hardened? And she's stick of being stereotyped as a princess and nothing else. I'm helping her break out of her stuffy prison."

"Well, just be careful you don't end up getting beheaded for treason like great uncle Eldorf."

"He was not our great uncle. Maybe ten greats ago.

Or fifteen. And that happened in Moldavia, not Altaleone."

"Still…chop chop."

"I'll mind my neck if you mind your business." He smiled, imagining his sister rolling her blue eyes, that familiar half-smile tugging at her expressive mouth. "But thanks for finding Signora Pazzi." He cleared his throat. Expressing emotion was hard for him but he was determined not to be like his dad, refusing to even feel anything after the loss of his wife during childbirth. "I love you."

"I love you too, big brother. And I hope you'll hook me up with some royal designs for my shop."

He laughed. "I'll do my best."

Lina decided to go to bed fairly early, and Beatriz headed to her room to sketch. Lorenzo hadn't texted her, and she decided their relationship was far enough along that she could make the first move in a text conversation.

How's your evening going? I'm working on some sketches.

She smiled. It was nice having someone you could text. And somehow keeping the relationship secret made it more delicious.

But when he hadn't responded five minutes later she decided her text was boring and stupid. He didn't want to waste time telling her how his evening was going. He was probably out with friends and doing something interesting. No doubt he didn't have time to respond to her banal message.

She got back to her sketches, which were for clothing to be worn in cooler weather. She was working on a midthigh length garment somewhere between a coat and a jacket when her phone buzzed.

She smiled, relieved, and picked it up, wondering what Lorenzo would respond. Instead it was from her mom and simply said, **Sandro shot.** Adrenaline surged through her, and she dived for the door and yanked it open. "Mom! Where are you?"

"Downstairs, come quick."

She pelted down to where her mom stood talking into her phone with three staff members nearby. She told one to get the car and another to phone ahead to make sure the route to the hospital was clear. Phone still in hand, Beatriz ran to the coat closet and retrieved coats for both of them. "What happened?"

She took her mom's arm, and they hurried out into the courtyard just as a driver brought a car up to the door. "Something went wrong." She looked around, glancing at the staff around them. "Someone with a gun." She was breathless and pale. "He's alive. A helicopter is flying him to the hospital."

Beatriz helped her into the back of the car, then dashed around to the other side. "How did this happen with Gibran there?"

"There was an avalanche and snow covered the road right after Sandro and Darias's car drove through the mountain pass."

"But there hasn't been an avalanche there in years."

"Gibran thinks someone dynamited to trigger it from high up the mountain."

"So the whole thing was planned." Beatriz couldn't believe it. "Why Sandro?"

"I don't know, sweetheart." Her mom gripped her hand. "I just pray he's not too badly hurt."

At the hospital they were ushered in by staff and

brought to an empty room to wait while he was in surgery. Soon Emma and Darias arrived, but no one knew where Serena was because she'd flown with Sandro in the helicopter and wasn't answering her phone.

"Is Serena a suspect?" asked Beatriz, suddenly aware that she was a virtual stranger in their midst.

"Oh, no, she saved his life," said Darias. "The shooter was Wilhelm, Dad's former valet."

"What?" Her mom looked shocked. "The blond boy? He's been with us for years."

"Yep." Darias's face was grave. "He's in custody. I trussed him myself and made sure the police had control of him before I left. Wilhelm was holding the gun to my head when Serena broke a window and distracted him and Sandro tackled him."

"Where was he shot?" her mom whispered.

"Upper arm and chest area," said Darias softly. "I'm going to see how the surgery's going."

"Okay." Their mom was doing her best to act calm and not cry, but Beatriz could see how upset she was. She herself felt numb and terrified at the same time. Sandro was the most happy-go-lucky of all of them—she couldn't imagine losing him. She slid her arm around her mom and squeezed her.

Darias soon came back, accompanied by a phalanx of nurses wheeling a wide-awake Sandro. Lina immediately burst into tears, and Beatriz had to bite her lip not to cry herself. Serena followed fast behind him and Sandro was lucid enough to propose marriage to her, which got everyone else in the room sobbing.

Beatriz was ready to collapse with relief that Sandro would be okay when suddenly her phone buzzed. **Evening is rather dull. Wish I was with you. I can't wait to see your drawings.**

Lorenzo! She'd forgotten all about him. She was about to text back—to fill him in on the evening's dramatic events—when something stopped her. If his evening was so dull, why did it take him over an hour to get back to her?

Maybe he was one of those guys whose affections cooled once he realized a girl really liked him. She hated playing games and was useless at them, but even she knew not to be too easily available.

Gibran wanted to know if there were any other staff members Wilhelm habitually spent time with and who else knew that the Cross of Blood meeting would take place at the lake house.

"No one knew." Darias frowned. "We only made the plans yesterday. I didn't even tell Sandro until today. I didn't mention it to a single member of staff. Wilhelm knew only because he drove us and he had less than an hour's warning."

"What happened to the regular driver?" asked Gibran.

"He came down with the stomach flu," said Darias.

"Maybe he was poisoned?" suggested Beatriz, her mind suddenly teeming with conspiracies.

"Could be." Gibran frowned. "Was there anyone else, outside of the Cross of Blood members—who we are now talking to—who knew of this meeting tonight?" He looked from Darias to Sandro to Serena to Emma to Lina to Beatriz.

I told Lorenzo. The thought assaulted her like a slap to the face. She hadn't given it a moment's thought at the time, but she'd told Lorenzo about the meeting and that it would be held at the lake house.

12

Beatriz held her breath, brain whirring with possibilities. Nina, the security guard, knew she had been with Lorenzo, but she didn't know Beatriz had mentioned the location of the meeting to him. Beatriz could say that she'd mentioned it in passing, but she knew that if she said anything in front of Darias he'd jump right down her throat and Lorenzo would suddenly be the prime suspect as the mastermind behind everything that had happened, including the murders.

What possible reason could Lorenzo have for wanting to hurt any of them? If anything, he could be accused of wanting to ingratiate himself into the family, not destroy it.

Lorenzo had nothing to do with this. She was sure of it.

The moment for her to say something passed, and she was pretty sure she managed to keep a neutral expression on her face.

Gibran turned to Darias. "This event is the perfect excuse for us to interview each member of the Cross of Blood. We now know all their identities and have made arrangements to follow up with them."

"I suppose that's one good thing that came out of

this. They'd always refused to reveal their identities under a five-hundred-year-old law protecting members of religious sects. Now hopefully we can get a better idea of what they're really all about. Their purported goal is protecting the monarchy, but not one of them tried to leap in and protect me."

"I think you should stay away from them from now on," said their mom, softly.

"I won't argue," said Sandro. He'd sunk back into the pillows, and Beatriz could see he was in pain.

"We should let Sandro rest," she said softly.

"Can I stay with him overnight?" asked Serena. She was still holding his uninjured hand and didn't look like she ever wanted to leave his side again.

"Of course," said Lina. "We'll have someone bring over a change of clothes and anything else you need."

"Not Wilhelm, though, okay?" said Sandro with a rough voice.

"No. Oh, goodness. I'd forgotten that the staff were involved. Maybe I'll just bring them myself."

"Don't worry, Mom. Katrina can bring them. I'd trust her with my life." Beatriz had known the chief of palace staff since she was her nanny many years ago.

"True. Thank goodness we know there's at least someone we can trust. I'd never have suspected Wilhelm. He seemed like such a nice boy."

"I wouldn't call him nice, Mom." Beatriz flashed back through memories of him. He wasn't the kind of person who stood out. "He was quiet and hardworking, which are not the same thing."

They all stood and promised to visit Sandro bright and early, then filed out of the room and were driven back to the palace. Beatriz was back in her room by the time she realized she never responded to Lorenzo. Not that she could have.

She picked up her phone. **Drawings were interrupted by my brother getting shot. Did you tell anyone there would be a meeting at the lake house tonight?**

She was about to send it, then realized that if anyone—such as Gibran—looked at her phone she'd as much as admitted that she told him about the meeting. She deleted the second sentence. She changed it to. **Luckily he's okay, but it's going to be hard to sleep tonight.**

He immediately texted back. **That's terrible. I'm so sorry. Glad he's okay.**

Then: **Did it happen at the lake house?**

She frowned. So much for her concern about secrecy. And the red flag of suspicion shot up in her brain. What was it with Lorenzo and the damn lake house? **Why do you ask?**

You told me your brothers were heading there.

I shouldn't have told you. It was supposed to be a secret. Did you tell anyone?

No. Are you okay? Would you like me to come keep you company?

What? Did he really think that would be a good idea right now? His arrogance defied belief, and she was more accustomed to arrogance than the next person. **No. Definitely not! Things are very tense here. Please do not come over.**

He was ballsy enough to come "surprise" her or something. Maybe her brothers were right, and he was someone to be wary of. Why was he so pushy?

Don't worry. I respect your privacy. Let me know when it's a good time to meet. I'll keep my

distance until you're ready.

She sighed. **Thanks. I'm sorry. I'm punchy tonight after everything that's happened. I'll be in touch.**

He responded. **In the meantime the memories of our last encounter will keep me warm. I miss you.**

Her chest tightened. She missed him too. Maybe she could just send him the drawing she did this morning, of the jacket or coat or whatever it was. She was proud of the lines and had some interesting ideas of what to make it out of. She was even thinking of making three versions—one metallicized leather, one trimmed with fur and one with feathers—simple classic lines, each with a bold texture.

Anyone but Lorenzo would think she was out of her mind to consider fashion at a time like this, but thinking about the coat soothed her. Design and creation were her happy place, and she hadn't fully realized that until Lorenzo came into her life.

I miss you too. I can't wait to see you again.

The next three days were fairly frantic, with visits to Sandro at the hospital, security grilling all the staff—some of whom had worked there longer than Beatriz had been alive and were in tears at beings suspects—and the flurry of feminine excitement over the prospect of Sandro and Serena's wedding.

Beatriz spent her spare time sketching and growing increasingly frustrated by her lack of practical skills. She knew some designers worked directly on the model, draping and pinning and cutting in a free-form manner that made each garment uniquely suited to both fabric and model.

For the first time in years, she found herself perusing the course catalog for the Instituto Marangoni. It was one of the finest fashion schools in the world, nearby in Milan. She imagined what it would be like to learn how to sew something herself, to experiment with stitches and seams and make alterations like a sculptor molding clay.

By day four she had a thick sheaf of sketches, and she was burning to show them to someone. She texted a few to Mari, who simply texted back **Cool!** She contemplated telling Mari about her planned show, but that seemed risky. What if Signora Pazzi turned up her very experienced nose at the designs? Or if, once fabricated, they looked terrible? Or, even worse, if Lorenzo simply lost interest and she was left on her own to plan and execute the show? She knew she'd never have the nerve to pull it off.

Much better to keep the whole plan secret. And she had no intention of mentioning Lorenzo to Mari. Her sister would want more details than she intended to divulge.

So she had to show the designs to Lorenzo.

He wanted to meet in town and suggested their usual rendezvous street—with her guard in tow. Beatriz didn't want to be out in public with the shooting still in the news, and she didn't want to go back to the Orangerie so soon.

So she suggested a visit to the lake house.

On a practical note, the house was her responsibility and she needed to see how much damage needed fixing. She knew a window had been broken during the altercation and boarded up, and Darias had warned her that the window had individual lead panes and would have to be handcrafted.

She also wanted to get a sense of whether she would want to do anything with the place. She barely remembered what it looked like, and since Lorenzo seemed so excited about it, he'd be the perfect person to visit with so she could see its advantages.

And she wanted to test him.

Would he disparage the place as a money pit that would cause her no end of trouble? Or would he launch into a litany of reasons why she should sell it to him? There was only one way to find out.

The gate to the lake property was chained shut, and Lorenzo's car was already at the side of the road outside the closed gate when she drove up, with Nina following close behind her. She waved to him and unlocked it, and he jumped out and pulled the heavy iron gates open. He looked striking as usual in dark pants and a wool coat, dark hair tossing in the breeze, and she had to fight an urge to kiss him in front of Nina.

The house itself looked grim. Even though there was no industrial pollution to blacken the stone and the roof and windows on the facade were intact, it had a dismal air of neglect. The style was odd to her eye—the simple lines and steep peaked roof of a mountain retreat, coupled with the grandeur and extravagant detail of a royal palace.

She pulled the big, old-fashioned key out of her pocket and unlocked the front door, which creaked open to reveal a large, dusty space that led into several other rooms.

"It's got wonderful light," exclaimed Lorenzo.

Beatriz laughed. "All the better to illuminate the dust mites." She closed the door behind them. Nina had stayed outside in the car. "Though it does have large windows."

Lorenzo took hold of her, pulled her close and kissed her until her belly quivered. "Much better," he said with a sigh when they finally pulled apart. "I've been aching for you."

"I've missed you too," she admitted. "I would have gotten away sooner if I could." And there was one thing she'd thought about almost as much as kissing Lorenzo. "Let me show you the drawings."

Lorenzo looked surprised, like he'd forgotten about the drawings, then he smiled. "I'd love to see them."

She had her folio in a satchel over her shoulder, and she walked through the empty house—which had very little furniture, only pieces too heavy to move easily—until she found the flat surface of a sun-faded billiard table. Heart pounding, she pulled out the drawings and spread them on the dull green surface. There were twenty in all, a mix of casual wear, outerwear and evening, but to her eye they had a distinct theme and really worked together.

She held her breath while Lorenzo contemplated them. "I like what you've done with the belted waist. It really pulls them all together." He looked up at her, grinning.

"Witty. But seriously, does it look passé?"

"I love it. There's no sexier silhouette."

She heaved a sigh of relief. "And I want to use a lot of leather. And feathers."

"Elegant." He picked up her jacket/coat picture and peered at it. "They look very wearable."

"They do, don't they?" She bit her lip. "Is that bad? At a lot of the shows I've been to the clothes are more conceptual and don't seem like something a real person would wear."

"Sometimes the designers do that just to get press. You won't need to do that."

"Why?"

He laughed. "Because you're you. A princess."

Her heart constricted. "I don't want that to be a selling point. If anything it will make people quick to dismiss me."

"But no one can ignore you, and if the clothes are good—and from what I can see the clothes will be great—you'll have a hit on your hands."

She drew in a shaky breath. "I wish I had your confidence."

"You should. You're very talented."

She shrugged, wishing she believed him. Maybe if the show went well she would have confidence in her abilities. "I do wish I could take some real classes and study design and sewing."

"You'd be surprised how many top designers didn't have a formal education."

"I suppose." She looked at all her drawings, most of them at least the tenth attempt, spread out on the old billiard table. She'd worked hard and was proud of her efforts but still felt like she was a baby attempting to run before she could walk. "But I was thinking…maybe I could do the degree at the fashion institute and then put together a show."

"What?" Lorenzo looked stunned again. "No way. Most people need to do that because they don't have the resources to simply create a collection. You do have those resources, and you'd be wasting your time to take a long series of courses. Signora Pazzi is the most accomplished seamstress in Milan. She has decades of accumulated wisdom, and I bet she never studied formally anywhere, either."

"I don't know." She rearranged a couple of the drawings. "It's a very short time to pull together twenty different looks. What if they're not done fast enough?"

"They will be. One of my favorite sayings in business is 'Where there's a will, there's a way.' If you're going to live your dreams you have to be bold enough to take that first step."

As if to demonstrate, he stepped forward and kissed her again. Her lips parted to welcome his and soon she'd melted into his arms again. Kissing Lorenzo made her feel invincible. With his strong body wrapped around hers she felt like she could take on the world—and win.

"Go for it," he whispered into her ear.

His hot breath further stimulated her senses. "I will." Chest filled with fresh confidence, she was ready to go shopping for fabrics right now.

"Excellent." Lorenzo pulled back. She felt his steamy gray gaze drift over her face, making her feel desirable as well as competent. "Now let's tour this old place."

Beatriz stiffened, and some of her suspicions crept back in. "Why are you so interested in this property?"

He shrugged. "I've only seen it from the outside before. You have to admit it's unusual."

"I suppose so. It was just built to be a summer house. It's never been lived in year round."

Lorenzo was already striding across the stone floor, into an adjacent room with the walls painted to look like inlaid marble. The paint was flaking off in some places.

She peered up at the high ceiling, where some paint hung like partially shed skin. "I should scrape back to the bare plaster and just repaint."

"I disagree. I love the worn aspect of the place. I feel like I'm in an ancient Roman temple in this room."

Beatriz squinted and tried to see the room from that perspective. She couldn't get past the peeling paint—probably filled with lead and who knows what else. "The floor is pretty." Made of actual inlaid marble, it was in great shape—hardly surprising since it was rarely walked on.

She strode ahead, walking through another two large rooms until she reached the big, empty gallery at the back of the building where the broken window had been boarded over with a bright yellow sheet of fresh plywood. She turned to Lorenzo. "I bet you enjoy the avant-garde aspect of this juxtaposition."

He laughed. "You already know me too well."

The windows were enormous and composed of individual panes held in lead frames. "Well, tough luck because I'm going to restore the window to its former glory."

The room was beautifully proportioned and the walls in relatively good condition, perhaps because it was on the north side of the house and suffered less from daily temperature changes.

"I'm glad to hear it." He looked around. "Think how this room would look with sleek modern furniture in it."

"It would be a stunning backdrop. The fireplace is so dramatic." Almost two stories high and made of carved pale stone, it grabbed her attention.

Soon she was striding through the house, noticing

details from wooden doors intricately carved with country scenes to the magnificent dining room, with its unusual made-in-place table still in residence. "I wonder what pictures hung here."

"The palace archives might have files of notes on it somewhere. But do you want to restore it to its former glory or reinvent it for the twenty-first century?"

"More yellow plywood?"

"I was thinking more along the lines of Le Corbusier."

"That's twentieth century." Why was he even thinking about what chairs would look good in her house? She decided to call his bluff and see how he reacted. She drew in a deep breath and screwed up her courage. His response could determine everything. "If you love the house so much and have such strong opinions about it, maybe I should rent it to you?"

13

Lorenzo stared at her. Her heart now thudded so hard she could hear her pulse pounding in her ears.

"Oh, no." His gaze held hers. "You must live here. This is an artist's house. It should be your canvas, your sanctuary. I'll count myself lucky if I'm invited to visit."

Beatriz swallowed as relief rolled through her in a hot wave.

"I'm not so sure, but I'll think about it." She looked around at the tall windows, lofty ceilings and the expansive view toward the nearby mountains. "It all seems so grand."

He laughed. "You live in what is arguably the grandest palace in Europe."

"I know. But I feel like I'm just one of the crowd there. It's not mine."

"And this house is. You could design and renovate it so that it's perfect for you. It's the ideal way to claim your independence. Lets go upstairs."

He led the way in his usual bold fashion and soon they were peering into the large, empty bedrooms. One was on a corner with a view over the lake from several large windows. The water shimmered like glass, perfectly reflecting the snowy mountains.

Beatriz wondered what it would be like to wake up to that view every morning. "This is a beautiful room."

"And it has an attached dressing room. Ideal for a fashion designer to store her personal collection."

Beatriz eyes widened. "I'm not going to wear them myself."

"Why not? You're the perfect advertisement for your unique style."

"Oh, I don't think so." She felt color rising to her cheeks. Lorenzo's gaze roved down over her physique. She wore a black turtleneck and black jeans, both more fitted than her usual attire because he'd given her confidence in her body.

Her nipples tightened, and she felt sensation ripple in her belly.

"It's a shame there's no bed in here." Lorenzo's low voice stirred something inside her.

"True. I think I'll have to fix that. I saw a stunning bed in white punched leather in Milan when we were walking around."

"I'm not a superstitious man, but I would take that as a sign." A smile tugged at his sensual mouth.

Beatriz had every intention of keeping her fashion work secret until the show, but there was no way she could keep her renovation project secret, so she quietly announced it to the family at dinner one night the next week. Sandro and Serena were still staying at the palace, waiting for his arm to improve enough for them to visit her family in Virginia, and Emma and Darias had come for dinner, as they often did.

"The lake house?" Her mom looked appalled. "But it's so remote. And dangerous."

"Just because bad things have happened there doesn't make it dangerous. It's time to reclaim it. Grandma wanted me to have the house, or she wouldn't have left it to me. I suspect she hoped I'd want to live there."

"I don't know, sweetheart." Her mom had put down her knife and fork. "What if you're all alone out there and something happens?"

"Maybe she won't be alone?" Liesel was still in residence at the palace, a circumstance Beatriz now deeply regretted bringing about. "Perhaps there are some other new developments you need to tell us about?"

"Nothing like that, no," she said too quickly. "But I am an adult and since there's no sign of me getting married and moving off to live with someone, I think it's time I struck out on my own."

"Oh, nonsense." Her mom stared at her. "Who told you such a thing? You're welcome to live here as long as you like. I love your company."

"And I love yours, but don't you think it's odd that I'm the oldest and I'm the only one who still lives at home?"

"I think it's a great idea," said Sandro. "Beatriz has an eye for art and design. Remember how she helped Dad plan the renovations for the Orangerie? That place was a hovel before she stepped in."

"I don't know why he ever bothered with that place," said her mom.

Beatriz was silent. Maybe they suspected him of using it to hide an affair, but no one would ever say it aloud. They loved their dad, and their mom, too much for that. "I did enjoy decorating the Orangerie, and the lake house has so much more potential. The views are unbelievable because it's so close to the mountains."

"Does Lorenzo Aldobrando have anything to do with this sudden interest in the lake house?" Darias had a suspicious expression on his face.

Beatriz was tempted to lie but why? If things kept going as well as they had been she'd surely go public with her relationship sooner or later. "I think his interest in it rather awakened my own. I never really thought about it before. But now that I've taken the time to look around the house and grounds, I can see that it would be a beautiful place to live."

"To live full time?" Their mom looked horrified. "But it's in the middle of nowhere."

"Hardly," said Sandro with a laugh. "Yes, it was a long horse-and-carriage ride when it was first built in the eighteen hundreds, but it's barely twenty minutes now."

"But there was an avalanche on the road!"

"Only because someone set dynamite there. Beatriz can arrange to have the snow load checked regularly and controlled with dynamite if needed."

Lina drew in a breath, looking very tense. "Gosh, I don't know. I suppose it makes sense on some levels but…"

"But you don't want to be left alone in your empty nest," said Liesel, coolly.

Lina blinked. "I suppose you're right. That sounds so selfish that I almost hate myself."

"You need to start dating, Mom." Sandro sipped his wine. "You're young and vibrant and have a lot of decades left to enjoy."

"Perish the thought." Lina grew pale. "I'll cherish the memory of your father until the day I die."

"Mom, that's just silly." Beatriz didn't like the idea of her mom being alone for decades any more than she wanted it for herself. "Even if you're not ready right now, you shouldn't rule the idea out altogether."

"I don't want to hear any mention of it again." Lina looked quite firm. "Let's change the subject. Will you build a riding arena at the lake house?"

"I don't know…" Beatriz hadn't really thought about actually living there and what that might entail. "I think I'll start with the inside and take things one step at a time."

The next two months were a flurry of activity. Beatriz hired tradesmen to fix up the lake house, which was well built and in surprisingly good condition considering its age. The bathrooms were outdated to the point of not being functional—no showers and toilets with tanks up near the ceiling—so Lorenzo helped her choose new fixtures befitting the dramatic and elegant setting.

The vast kitchen was not very user-friendly but was so cool-looking that they managed to sneak in a few useful modern appliances without changing the overall appearance of the room too much.

Beatriz ended up using colors from the view—the ice caps on the mountains, the reflection of pine trees in the lake, the afternoon sun dancing on the water—to inspire paint colors for the rooms. Soon the house was a freshly restored blank canvas ready for decorating.

Lorenzo had furnished numerous upscale residences as part of his real estate business, so he took her to showrooms and helped arrange delivery of a variety of sleek and dramatic pieces that perfectly offset their ornate setting. In less than eight weeks it was ready for her to move in.

The house renovation gave her a wonderful excuse to be gone from the palace for extended periods of time, which allowed her to travel to Milan and meet with Signora Pazzi and work on bringing her designs to life.

Lorenzo often met her there, and despite her constant tail of security, they began to spend regular steamy afternoons in his comfortable apartment.

"I've never been so happy!" she exclaimed, breathless, after a magical round of lovemaking. "I spend my whole day dreaming and creating."

"And driving," he teased. "I'm happy that you took a chance on yourself. Look at what you're capable of."

"Right? I had no idea. Seriously, I would never have attempted either the fashion or the renovation by myself."

"You just needed some gentle prodding."

"Like my horse when I'm trying to teach him a new dressage movement. He doesn't realize he has it in him until I convince him."

Lorenzo kissed her softly on the forehead. "I'm glad you trusted me. Sooner or later your family will trust me as well."

Beatriz sighed. "I don't know. They're stubborn as mules."

"And they haven't been asking what you're up to?"

"I suppose I've been deflecting them effectively to avoid conflict and they've rather given up. Mama says I seem like I'm in a good mood all the time. I had to agree because she's right." She stroked Lorenzo's tousled hair.

"You're finally using your creative talents, and I'm keeping you satisfied in bed. It's a heady combination." He nibbled on her earlobe, which they'd both discovered was a powerful erogenous zone for her. "When are you moving into the lake house?"

Beatriz stomach tightened. "I don't know. I'm nervous about it."

"Why? It'll be perfect. I can come stay there every night with you."

She stared. They hadn't talked about this before. She'd had visions of being all alone there—not including the ubiquitous security presence—and startling at shadows in the nighttime. "You would?"

"Absolutely. Why do you think I encouraged you to carve out your own space away from the prying eyes of the palace? I love spending stolen afternoons with you, but I want more."

More. What exactly did that entail? She knew that at this point they were officially dating. A story about them, complete with pictures of them kissing over cappuccinos in an unguarded moment at an outdoor café, had been published in one of the paparazzo magazines and on royal gossip websites.

Far from being horrified at the intrusion, Beatriz welcomed the newly public aspect of her relationship. If her family couldn't accept that she was seeing Lorenzo, at least other people could. And there had been no mention of the stupid ancient feud between their families because likely no one outside the two families even remembered it.

Although she normally shied away from press stories about the family, this one had made her proud that for once she wasn't the lonely cloistered princess that no one loved.

She was ready for *more*.

If anyone in the family had read the article they hadn't said a word. But since they had a family policy of avoiding paparazzi gossip, they might not have seen it at all. It was ridiculous that the general public knew more about her relationship with Lorenzo than her own family.

"Let me talk to Mama about it. I don't want her to be lonely. Maybe I could do something where I spend weekdays in one place and weekends at another?"

"That sounds like a good start." Lorenzo moved his face over her belly and fluttered kisses over it until she grew so aroused she could barely stand it. She could hardly imagine what it would feel like to fall asleep in his arms and wake up in them in the morning.

And she was ready to find out.

But it was ridiculously hard to break the news to her mom. For the third night in a row they sat alone at the large dinner table and her mom was rambling on about the burgeoning plans for Sandro and Serena's wedding. "Signor Haas will make the cake of course, but he told me he can't design it until he has some idea of the number of guests, and I've been asking them for weeks and they won't give me a list."

"Don't worry, it will come together. They're busy."

"And Serena's aunt wants to make her dress." Lina raised her eyebrows. "Which is super sweet, but does she have any idea of the kind of scrutiny a royal wedding dress will be subjected to?"

"Mom, Serena is a social media star. Trust me, she knows. I'm sure her aunt is very talented. Don't worry about it."

"I can't help myself. I'm worrying about everything these days. I have too much time on my hands."

Beatriz inhaled silently. Once again this was hardly the ideal moment to bring up moving out of the palace. But there was never going to be a good time.

"The renovations on the lake house are almost done. I'm going to move some things over there and spend a little time there. Just a few days." She said it as fast as she could, with emphasis that it wasn't going to be a permanent move.

Not yet, at least.

Her mom stared at her. "All by yourself? But, sweetheart, why?"

Beatriz swallowed. She hated lying to her mom, or at least not telling the whole truth, and sooner or later her mom would hear about it from Liesel, who checked the gossip websites and would find the article about them. "I'll have a security guard there, of course." She inhaled and screwed up her courage. "And Lorenzo will spend some time there with me."

Her mom looked poleaxed. "Lorenzo…Aldobrando? Have you been…has he.… What's going on?"

"We're dating." She tried for a pleasantly cheerful facial expression. Like a normal person telling her mom she was dating a man.

"But Darias warned you about him." Her mom seemed to have forgotten all about her meal. "He's up to something. He's always wanted that lake house, and now…"

"Mom, he's not trying to get his hands on the house." Exasperation rose inside her. "Why do you all think it's so impossible that he could be interested in *me*? Why is that so hard to believe?"

Her mom frowned and waved her hands in the air. "Oh, no, sweetheart, that's not what I meant at all. But a girl in your position does have to be careful and question a man's motives."

"He likes me, Mom. We've been spending a lot of time together." She wished she could fess up about the fashion designs, but she was too afraid that her mom would take it as disrespectful defiance of her dad's opinion or—worse yet—that she would think it an awful idea and try to dissuade Beatriz from going through with it.

It was hard enough to keep forging ahead when her own ego was her worst enemy; she wasn't sure she could push through a wall of negativity from her best friend and staunchest supporter.

Her mom still hadn't spoken. She'd picked up her spoon and started playing with her carrot and beet soup.

"He's lovely, Mom. Seriously, he's not at all the way everyone thinks he is. He's creative and thoughtful...and a great kisser."

Her mom looked up, startled. "You kissed him?"

"Mom, you're acting like I'm sixteen. I'm a grown woman. I've done more than kiss him." She took a swig of wine. "I wish you'd all stop treating me like a baby. I'm the same age as Darias, and he's apparently trusted with ruling this country. No one even trusts me to go on a date by myself."

"We just care about you, my love."

"Really? I feel like everyone just wants me to stay quietly out of the way and avoid embarrassing the family. Just because I'm not a genius scientist or a hotshot lawyer doesn't mean I don't still have hopes and dreams just like my brothers and sisters."

"Of course you do." Her mom's spoon drifted down to her dish again without actually reaching her mouth. "And I realize that I've been taking you too much for granted. You must invite Lorenzo here for dinner with us. Darias and Emma can come over, and we can all get to know him better."

Apprehension spiked inside Beatriz, but she shoved it aside. "That would be a great idea. I'm sure he'd like that."

"Wonderful. Let's plan it for next week. You tell me what day is good for him, and we'll set it all up." Her mom's smile looked forced. As a professional princess, her mom was very skilled at hiding her emotions and looking pleased all the time, but Beatriz could see right through it. Her mom still hated the idea of her being with Lorenzo.

"At least give him the benefit of the doubt, okay?" She didn't want her family ganging up on him.

"I promise. We'll welcome him with open arms." Another fake smile. "So, uh, when were you thinking of staying over at the lake house?"

"Tomorrow night." She wanted to make her move before she chickened out. That strategy seemed to be working for her lately. "I'll just pack a few things and give it a try. I already spoke to Gibran, and Nina will stay there with me."

"And Lorenzo will be there?" Her mom asked cheerfully, as if she didn't care one way or the other. Again, Beatriz saw right through her act.

"I don't know. I haven't asked him. I'll be fine there by myself, don't worry."

She could tell her mom was thinking about the

murders and the shooting incident with Sandro. "It's totally renovated now. It looks fresh and new everywhere. And a firm from Zurich installed a new state-of-the-art security system that monitors heat and movement. It would be impossible for anyone to break in undetected. I'll be fine. And so will you."

Her mom smiled. "I will. I don't want to be a drag on you. I'm sorry I've been so clingy lately; it's just that I'm so used to having your father to talk to."

"I understand, Mom. I really do. And I'm going to join the chorus saying that when you're ready you really should think about dating again."

Her mom laughed, but this time it was a hollow laugh that really wasn't intended to sound charming. "Who would I date at my age? I doubt I could even accept an invitation without wondering what he was up to. I suppose that's why I worry about you."

"You didn't date dad for his title or money."

"I didn't care about those things, but my family did. They all but arranged our marriage for me. I barely had a say in the matter."

"Really?" Beatriz had never heard this before. The family legend was of heated glances across a crowded ballroom. "I thought you met by chance."

Her mom smiled. "Nope. My formidable Aunt Friedl, who was five feet tall and married to a duke, orchestrated the whole thing. She convinced Emil's father that I was a perfect, virginal royal bride with just enough blue blood to be suitable but not so much as to be too demanding. It was all signed, sealed and delivered within two months."

Beatriz stared. Her mom picked up her soup spoon, and this time she ate. "Did you fall in love with Dad?" She couldn't help asking. Her whole vision of their family had been turned on its head.

"Oh, yes. We grew fond of each other very quickly. He was a warm man and always caring and attentive. I had no complaints."

That did not sound like the kind of passion a girl hoped for—or the kind that Beatriz enjoyed with Lorenzo. Just thinking about him made her blood heat and her palms tingle.

"Did you ever love anyone else? Before him, I mean?"

Her mom looked up for a moment, and a distant look made her eyes glitter. "There was someone once. A long time ago. It would never have worked out, though. I was lucky to have met your father. He was a wonderful husband."

"I miss Dad so much." Beatriz sighed. "I miss riding with him and hearing him ramble on about his day of shooting or his new litter of hounds."

"Me too, sweetheart. It's hard to go on without him, but we have to."

Beatriz wondered if her mom ever suspected her dad of cheating. She'd rather die than bring it up. What good would that do? "I wonder why Dad never pressured me to date or marry anyone. If anything he just found fault with any man who even looked at me."

"I suspect he didn't like the idea of anyone stealing his little princess. You were always your father's favorite, though don't tell your siblings."

Beatriz sighed. She knew it too. She and her dad had so much in common—they both preferred to be out on horseback or in front of the library fire to making waves in the world of science or law. They were both old-school royals in a way her other siblings weren't. "He'd have been very suspicious of Lorenzo, wouldn't he?"

Her mom smiled. "Very. In fact, he might even have challenged him to pistols at dawn if he suspected him of kissing you without an official engagement in place." They both laughed.

Beatriz reflected that Lorenzo might never have been daring enough to approach her if her father was still alive. And he'd never have had the opportunity to court her so boldly at Darias's coronation. "But you'll give him a chance, though, right?"

"Absolutely. I look forward to getting to know him." Her mom smiled warmly. "And I'll encourage Darias to keep his sword sheathed as well."

"I appreciate it." Beatriz felt a flutter of nerves when she thought about Lorenzo sitting down with her family. She wasn't ready to reveal her secret fashion project, and she didn't want them to know she'd already made love with him. The entire dinner would involve tiptoeing around the truth in a way that made her thoroughly uncomfortable.

But if it went well she and Lorenzo would be officially dating, and perhaps even on the way to something more permanent....

14

Beatriz paced around her big house, admiring the fine original finishes—inlaid marble floors, carved wood and the tall windows—but still feeling out of place. Nina was settled into the comfortable staff suite on the first floor, with a view of monitors in several locations. So she wasn't really alone, and she certainly wasn't in danger.

But she couldn't help a vague feeling of unease. She'd never seen the murder scenes involving her father and grandmother, or even glimpsed pictures of them, but that didn't stop her imagination from running away with her.

Where's Lorenzo? He'd said he'd come tonight, but it was already seven and had been dark for some time. He hadn't called or texted, and she didn't want to be pushy or seem insecure by contacting him.

Her phone pinged, and she sighed with relief. Maybe he got stuck in a meeting and was running late. **How does it feel to be in the place where your father died? You're next.** She shrieked and dropped the phone. Then grabbed it and called Nina. Her hands were shaking so hard it took several tries.

Nina came running up the stairs and was in the library in less than two minutes. "Let me see."

Beatriz handed her the phone. She peered at the text and contacted Gibran with the number. "He'll run it right now."

"It's a different number than the person who texted me before."

"It could still be the same person."

"Who knows I'm here?"

"The staff." She lifted a brow. "We've been unable to root out any accomplices to Wilhelm, and he swears there aren't any, but everyone is under suspicion."

"Why would they want to kill me?" She hated how scared she sounded.

"I can't imagine. They're probably just trying to scare you. There's no one on the premises, that I'm sure of. We'd know if a mouse snuck in—our body-heat detectors are that sensitive."

"I feel like I should respond." Beatriz didn't want to give this jerk the last word.

"And say what?" Nina looked wary.

"That he's a coward. Hiding behind a phone." Anger surged in her, fury that someone got entertainment out of trying to scare her.

"Better not to," said Nina softly. "I understand the urge, but you don't want to provoke them."

"Don't I? Maybe it will draw him out into the open, where we can deal with him."

The both stopped at the sound of a car. Her heart quickened. Lorenzo? Or someone else, possibly the anonymous texter.

Nina put Beatriz's phone down and pulled a gun from a holster on her ankle, which surprised Beatriz as she had no idea Nina carried one. "Stay here. I'll see who it is."

"It might be Lorenzo." She didn't want him to get shot. Disobeying Nina's order, she followed her to the front hallway downstairs and peered through the window next to the door.

Sure enough, Lorenzo's blue Audi sat in the drive. "It's just Lorenzo" she called to Nina. Nina stared out the window, watching with her gun in her hand as if Lorenzo might suddenly open fire. "You can put the gun away."

Nina hesitated for a moment, then tucked it back into her ankle. "You know how to reach me if you need me.."

"Yes, thank you." Did Nina suspect Lorenzo? Never mind, she didn't want to think about that now.

Lorenzo bounded up the front steps with a grin on his face. "The place looks amazing with lights blazing in the windows! Have you settled in?"

"Kind of." She kissed him, but she was still tense after the unpleasant surprise. "I don't feel at home yet."

"That will take time. Are you okay? You look pale."

"I'm fine." She didn't really want to tell him about the new text. What if he freaked out and wanted to investigate immediately? Still, it was a relief that he was here. She felt safe in Lorenzo's confident, muscular presence.

He'd made her feel safe the last time too, in the woods outside the town. It suddenly struck her that she'd been about to meet Lorenzo both times the texter contacted her. How odd.

"Beatriz, what's going on?" He must have read something in her expression. "Is it bothering you that your relatives died here?"

"No," she said firmly. "If anything that makes me more determined to reclaim the place and live in it. To defy the people who tried to destroy our family." She drew in a shaky breath. "But I got another stupid text. Someone trying to make me feel uneasy."

"Looks like they succeeded." He drew her into his arms and kissed her forehead. She let out a sigh and sank into him.

"Not really, I'm more angry than anything." She hugged him close. "I think that now I'm finally stepping outside my comfort zone and taking chances I don't feel as powerless as I used to. I actually wish the person would come forward instead of skulking around."

"Did you report it?"

"Yes."

"Good." Lorenzo kissed her softly, then harder, which made her knees weaken. "Because we have more important things to deal with. I'm making you dinner."

She glanced at the bags he'd brought in from the car. An overnight bag and a dark canvas bag. "You're a genius. I was so anxious about staying overnight here and leaving my mom alone at the palace that I only brought a few things. I could have made an omelet, but that's about it."

"Let's head to the kitchen." His mischievous grin made her stomach tingle with something other than hunger. Within half an hour he'd seared two thin steaks, sautéed a mix of tender baby vegetables and poured them both big glasses of red wine. As she sipped the wine Beatriz began to relax into her new surroundings.

They ate their dinner in the big dining room, with

its art nouveau–style stained glass windows and massive carved table, and afterward she was so relaxed she decided to say what was still nagging at the back of her mind. "The jerk who texted me mentioned the murder of my father and grandmother, then said, 'You're next.' " She frowned. "Why would someone want to kill me?"

Lorenzo's brow furrowed "Would you inherit the throne if something happened to Darias?"

"No. Females only inherit if there's no male heir. My grandmother was the oldest of three daughters. If something happened to Darias—perish the thought—Sandro would be the heir."

"Hence the conspirators' desire to attack them both."

Beatriz stared at him. How did he know about the incident? She must have mentioned it to him. Gibran had gone to some pains to keep it out of the press. She'd told him that Darias and Sandro were coming here, then later than Sandro was injured protecting Darias, so he must have put two and two together.

But if she couldn't talk to Lorenzo about this stuff, who could she talk to?

"But what do they hope to achieve? Wilhelm, the guy who did it, turned out to be some disgruntled former aristocrat whose ancestors had been sent into exile. Does he think that if they could kill off all ten of us they could somehow take over the country? It doesn't add up."

Lorenzo poured more wine into her glass. "I doubt it's that simple. People these days are more interested in money than the trappings of aristocracy."

"I agree, so the people who kidnapped Emma to

get a bank code made a lot more sense. Why is someone texting me just to weird me out?"

Lorenzo got up from his chair and came around the table. Before she could protest he picked her up in his arms. "First they're going to have to get through me."

She felt a smile spread over her face. How could he pick her up so easily? She loved how strong he was. "You do make me feel safe."

"And you make me feel very protective." He kissed her, still holding her up in the air. "In fact, I'd like to stow you safely away in bed for the night."

She giggled. "Shouldn't we clean up first?"

"Don't you have servants for that?" Lorenzo lifted a brow. She couldn't tell if he was joking.

"Well, actually Lori will come in the morning to do the daily cleaning."

"Problem solved." He grabbed both their wine glasses, without putting her down, and headed for the stairs.

"How can you carry me so easily?"

"You're light as a feather." He strode up the stairs as if she were weightless and headed down the hallway to her room.

"You remember which one is mine?"

"Of course." He opened the door and swept her inside. She'd left the lights on—the eeriness of an unfamiliar house after dark had made her turn lights on everywhere—and the room glowed. The dark wood of the lovely bed he'd helped her choose contrasted with the soft white of the textured bedding and the warm amber of the art deco lamps. "It looks beautiful."

"Doesn't it? It feels much more me than my room

at the palace. Even though I've slept in there since I was a baby, it was decorated for some ancient ancestor and no one even thought to update the brocade fabric on the walls or the ten feet of velvet curtains. I feel like I've been staying overnight in someone else's room my whole life and now I'm finally in my own space."

Still holding her in his arms, he kissed her cheek. "Welcome home."

"I give you full credit. I don't think it would have even crossed my mind to live here."

"And now you do." He laid her gently down on the soft bedding.

"Not officially. I told my mom I was staying for a day or two. I didn't want to freak her out."

"I'm sure she's just fine." Lorenzo joined her on the bed, and they lay side by side. End-of-day stubble ornamented his chiseled jaw. "Maybe she's even celebrating you seizing some independence."

Suddenly Beatriz remembered the dinner plans she'd made with her mom. "She'd like you to come for dinner with us next week. I think Darias and Emma will be there too."

"I'd love to."

"Hopefully Darias won't challenge you to another joust."

"If he does, I'll make sure to win this time." His mischievous grin reassured her that he was joking. "I'm looking forward to getting to know your family better."

"That's what my mom said. I think it's silly that I've had to keep you a virtual secret so far. We're both grown adults and have nothing to do with what happened hundreds of years ago. Not that I even know what all the fuss was about."

"Me either. Who cares? Let's live in the present."

They kissed until the scent and the taste of him overwhelmed her senses, then they tore off each other's clothes, laughing, and made hot, steamy, passionate love on her brand-new white sheets.

Afterward they lay in each other's arms, and Beatriz sighed. Everything was so perfect. Lorenzo fulfilled her more than she'd ever dreamed, and their relationship was on the way to some sort of official status. Her fashion designs had exceeded her expectations, and she was excited about seeing them come to life. And now she was building a real, grown-up life for herself in this lovely house overlooking the most beautiful lake in Altaleone.

Could things get any better than this?

Two days later it was Monday morning, and Lorenzo lay next to Beatriz in her spacious bed. For a while he watched her sleep, resisting the urge to stroke her long hair. He didn't want to get up and go to the investor meeting in Turin, but the deal had been in the works for months and he wasn't going to blow it, even for a woman as enchanting—and royal—as Beatriz.

As he dressed he reflected what his ancestors, who'd been smarting over the loss of this property for hundreds of years, would think if they could see him climb out of bed in it this morning. Would they be laughing that an Aldobrando had flirted and wooed his way back onto the stunning acreage his forbears had once called home?

He kissed Beatriz goodbye and they arranged to meet in Milan on Wednesday, when she'd be coming into the city to work with Signora Pazzi. He heard her phone ring as he hurried downstairs, already on the way to being late. It was hard to leave Beatriz. Something about her made him want to hold her in his arms and whisper sweet nothings to her just to see a smile brighten her habitual serious expression.

He climbed into his car and drove to the new gate that had been installed. There was an elaborate code—which changed every day—to enter but to leave he only had to press a button. The gate had just closed behind him when his phone rang with an unfamiliar number.

"Hello."

"Lorenzo Aldobrando?"

"Speaking."

"This is Gibran Al Nazariyah. I work for the Leone family."

"Yes, Beatriz has mentioned you. You're the head of security, right?" A twinge of anxiety suddenly tugged at him. "Is Beatriz okay?"

"Oh, yes, absolutely." There was a pause. "But she's mentioned that she received another text from an unknown individual."

"Yes. I do hope you catch them soon."

"And that she was waiting to meet you both times she received the texts."

"That is an odd coincidence." Lorenzo's pulse picked up. Would they try to make something of it? He had no idea why the person had chosen to contact her when she was on her way to meet them.

"I think so too." Another pause, long enough to become uncomfortable. "I'd like to interview you at the palace."

Lorenzo frowned. "Interview? Do you mean

question me?"

"Yes, exactly."

Indignation surged in his gut. He wasn't a common criminal—or even a suspect—to be questioned and cross-questioned. Still, he didn't want to rub Beatriz's family the wrong way. "I've been invited for dinner at the palace this week. Thursday, in fact. I could meet with you then."

More silence. This Gibran character knew how to make you sweat. "I'd prefer to do it before then. Tomorrow at the latest."

"I'm afraid that won't be possible. I have a meeting in Turin today, then I'm traveling to Rome for another meeting tomorrow."

"You can cancel one of them." No hesitation now. "It's important that I meet with you as soon as possible."

Lorenzo took the turn toward the main road, thoughts racing through his head. "Am I a suspect?"

"Until we have more information, everyone is a suspect."

Lorenzo frowned. If he was a suspect he needed to call a lawyer—now. "I'll call you back."

He hung up and called the lawyer who handled his more acrimonious real estate transactions, who in turn suggested a well-known criminal lawyer based in Altaleone. Lorenzo explained the situation, and the lawyer assured him that they had no grounds whatsoever to question him about anything and that he would handle it.

Then he called Beatriz.

15

"Hi, sweetie." There was a question in her voice. Beatriz must be surprised that he was calling when he'd left her barely an hour ago.

"Gibran just asked me to come in for an interview."

"Don't worry about it. It's a formality. We all know you didn't do anything. It's just so they can cross you off their list."

Lorenzo hesitated. He was still driving, just now reaching the outskirts of Milan. Had he made a mistake to put up resistance? "But why would I even cross their minds?"

"Because I told Gibran that I was about to meet you both times the texter contacted me. I told him it was just a coincidence. You're not worried, are you?" She sounded anxious.

"No, of course not." Now he was worried. The family already hated him for the sins of his ancestors, and might latch onto any excuse to put him out of reach of their beloved Beatriz. Putting him behind bars for treason and murder would be an effective way to achieve their goals. "But why did you tell him that?"

"I didn't, really. It just came out when he was

asking me about the circumstances surrounding the texts."

"I bet Gibran is embarrassed that they still don't even have a solid suspect in the murders that happened last summer. He's clutching at straws." He couldn't keep the anger out of his voice. "I'm a respectable citizen, and I've never committed a crime in my life. He has literally no grounds whatsoever to suspect me."

"I agree." She sounded tense. "That's what I told him."

"Your family doesn't want me seeing you."

"I'm not sure they even know about this. It was a conversation I had directly with Gibran. He's charged with keeping me safe—with keeping all of us safe."

"They know. Trust me." Indignation tightened his muscles. If he wanted to, he could probably talk Beatriz into selling the damn house to him right now. Yes, she'd decorated it her way but wouldn't she prefer a different castle without bloodstains scrubbed out of the floor? Perhaps a beautiful ancient palazzo in Milan, near the fashion scene and away from the clutches of her overprotective family?

But he had feelings for her, dammit. And he wanted to see her have that show they'd dreamed and schemed together.

He drove into the city center. "I called a lawyer."

"What!? Why?"

"Gibran said I'm a suspect."

"I don't believe it." Alarm made her voice shrill.

"Ask him." Yes, Gibran had said "everybody" was a suspect, but Lorenzo wasn't gullible enough to fall for that. "I'm a prominent businessman, and I don't take kindly to having my reputation tarnished by false accusations." He tried to keep his voice steady and calm while anger simmered inside him. "The lawyer agreed with me."

"Oh."

He hoped his lawyer would get him out of talking to Gibran or his goons, but there was no way to be sure. He was dealing with royals after all. "I'd better go. I need to park and get to my meeting. I just wanted to give you a heads up on the situation. I suspect your family won't want me to come for dinner now."

He instantly regretted that rather snippy statement, true though it likely was.

"I'm sure they will. Don't worry about it. I'll talk to them." Doubt shimmered in her voice. "I miss you."

"I miss you too." He said it softly, careful to keep his anger out of his voice. "You're the best thing that ever happened to me, Beatriz." He had to be careful that this unexpected snafu didn't drive a wedge between them. If Beatriz had to choose between him and her family, he'd be stupid to think she'd choose him.

"And you're the best thing that has ever happened to me by a really long way." She sounded emotional.

"I wish I was there to give you a hug and tell you it will all be fine."

"It will all be fine," she said with gusto. "I'm sure of it. Have a good meeting, and I'll talk to you tonight."

They hung up with the usual romantic pleasantries, and Lorenzo headed into his meeting still seething with indignant rage. Just because he'd dared to kiss their precious princess they thought he should now be subjected to interrogation and possible false charges?

In the old days they'd have locked him in a tower somewhere and left him to rot without trial. They might be royal, but this was the twenty-first century and they'd better wake up and smell the legal briefs.

Beatriz drove to the palace as fast as she could, with Nina in hot pursuit. Her mom was in the living room and rushed toward her with a big smile as soon as she saw her. "You're back! Wonderful. Darias and Emma will be here any moment." Beatriz could tell she was putting a brave face on and had missed her terribly. She hugged her mom.

But she was too upset to hold back. "Mama, Gibran wants to interrogate Lorenzo. He thinks he's a suspect!"

Her mom stared. "In what?"

"I don't know exactly." She hadn't told her mom about the texts. She didn't want to alarm her.

"Not the murders." Her mom's face tightened. "Lorenzo? Why would he…?"

"I don't know what it's about. But as you can imagine he's really upset."

"Who's really upset?" Darias strode through the door and pulled off his scarf and coat. Emma came right behind him.

Beatriz's mom looked at her. "Lorenzo. Because Gibran wants to question him."

"Gibran hasn't interviewed him yet? Why not?" Darias gave his mom a kiss on the cheek like this whole conversation had little importance either way.

"Why would he?" Beatriz hated the squeaky indignation in her voice. "What has Lorenzo ever done to anyone in this family? He even agreed to let you conquer him in that dumb joust."

"That was magnanimous of him, I admit, but I'm with Gibran in thinking that everyone is a suspect until proven otherwise. Especially anyone who's becoming increasingly intimate with my sister."

"We're not becoming increasingly intimate; we're actually dating." It was time her brother realized that she and Lorenzo were an item, not just a pointless flirtation. "He just spent the weekend with me."

"So that's why you wanted to renovate that house." Darias raised a brow. "It all makes sense now. And I'm sure it's a total coincidence that the house he's spending time with you in is the one he tried—in vain—to acquire from me before he realized it was actually yours." His voice dripped with sarcasm.

"Darias!" His mom touched his arm.

"It's insulting that you assume a man would only be interested in me for my real estate. As it happens we're—" She wanted to say that they were in love, but she couldn't vouch 100 percent for his feelings. Or even her own. She was naturally wary, but she was pretty sure they were heading in the love direction. "We're very close."

Darias sat down on the sofa. "If he has nothing to hide, then he won't mind talking to Gibran."

"But he does mind." Beatriz hated his casual attitude. These days he was acting more like her father than her—technically—younger brother. "It's an assault on his character. He's done nothing whatsoever that could cause him to be a suspect."

"Except for spending time with you." Darias lifted a brow. "You have to admit that anyone making an effort to get close to the Leone family has to be suspected of trying to infiltrate and possibly undermine us. And Gibran said that you were about to meet him both times that you received hostile texts."

"What hostile texts?" Her mom and Emma spoke at the same time.

Beatriz scowled at Darias. Then looked at her mom. "Silly idle threats that could have been sent by anyone. What would Lorenzo gain from doing that?"

Darias stretched out. "Perhaps he wanted to scare you. Then he could rush in and be the valiant hero rescuing the damsel in distress."

"What rubbish." Beatriz protested, but a teeny part of her remembered that getting the creepy texts did make the shelter of his strong arms that much more comforting. "I'm confident he had nothing to do with those texts. And I'd just invited him to eat with us on Thursday. He was looking forward to getting to know you all and putting all that foolish family history nonsense behind us, and now this. It's embarrassing."

"Darling, these are not normal times," said her mom. "Enough has happened that we have to put safety above etiquette. I'm sure it will go smoothly, and then we can all put it behind us and enjoy a nice dinner on Thursday."

Beatriz inhaled deeply. "I suppose so." Lorenzo wouldn't really refuse to be interviewed, would he? Darias had a point. If he had nothing to hide, then why worry?

"Are we ever going to get to see all your gorgeous renovations?" asked Emma, in an obvious effort to change the subject.

"Would you like to?" Beatriz hadn't suggested it because people seemed overwhelmed with opinions whenever the lake house came up. "I know you all thought I was crazy to do it up, but I think you'll see it differently now."

"I'd love to see it." Emma clapped her hands together. "And Darias would too. Wouldn't you?" She kissed him playfully on the cheek.

He glowered a bit. "I wouldn't mind. The last two times I've been there it was a recent crime scene so I have a rather negative impression of the place."

"Don't worry, we got most of the blood out of the floors," quipped Beatriz. "And if you dwell on that, then you're letting the criminals win. It's a beautiful old house that deserves to be lived in and enjoyed."

"I agree," said Lina. "We can't let evil people sour and destroy a fine old estate. I think Beatriz was right to reclaim it and put her stamp on it."

Beatriz smiled. Her mom was being sweet. She'd called the lake house a "grim old barrack of a place" more than once. "How about this afternoon?"

"But you just got back!" her mom protested.

"It's really not that far. Only twenty minutes. We can have lunch in town and then head out there." The idea had seized her, and now she wanted to share her new creation. She suddenly wondered if she'd left any of her designs lying around in her bedroom.

Probably.

But maybe it was time to begin sharing that dream too? She'd come out about her relationship with Lorenzo, she'd claimed her right to make a home for herself, and now she could show them her creative side as well. Suddenly her life was blossoming with potential—like her brothers' and sisters'—and she had a wonderful feeling that the sky was the limit on her ambitions.

"All right, let's do it," said Darias gruffly. "I could go for a plate of old man Andres's schnitzel. I have to meet with the vineyard manager at four, but I'll be back by then."

Emma grinned at Beatriz. "I can't wait to see what you've done. I only saw it that one night—when Sandro got shot—and it was dark and gloomy and mysterious."

"It's still rather mysterious—the lake has that effect—but it's no longer gloomy. The windows are huge and fill all the rooms with light."

"Or moonlight," muttered Darias.

"It sounds marvelous, sweetheart," said her mom. "Now let me think, what can I bring as a housewarming gift?"

They ate a luxurious lunch at a restaurant old enough for their great-great-great-grandparents to have dined there, then headed off to the lake house in two cars. Spring was in full effect, with lush green grass carpeting the meadows and tiny wildflowers scattered across them like confetti.

The drive to the lake house was a climb into the mountains, where the last of the winter's snow still clung to the highest peaks. Even the road was improved. Beatriz suspected Darias of arranging that on the sly when he heard she was driving out there so much.

"Here it is." Nina and the security guards that monitored Darias, Emma and her mom all rushed out to open the gate before she could climb out of the car. The drive went along the lake, where they all oohed and ahhed over the dramatic way it reflected the mountains around it, toward the house.

"I never noticed how beautiful it is here," exclaimed Lina, as they approached.

"C'mon, Mom," said Darias. "You haven't been here in fifteen years."

"Possibly not. I'm not sure I've ever been inside. Your father had pheasant shoots here from time to time so I stood around and froze outside the place."

"Yes, I got to know the estate from hunting here with Dad." Beatriz remembered how much she'd loved those icy mornings when the horses came off the truck with steam pouring out of their nostrils. "It reminds me of the happy times we spent together."

They pulled up in front of the house, and she gave them a tour, pointing out all the historic details and explaining her choice of paint colors and upholstery and furnishings.

"I'm floored," her mom said. "It's so stunning. Each room is just perfection. You took a dark old house that nobody wanted and made it fresh and modern and inviting."

"You have a lot of talent," said Emma. "You could be a decorator."

"Oh, I just had fun with it." Beatriz beamed inwardly. They had no idea that she planned to be far more than a decorator. If all went well her clothing could be in stores in just a few months.

She had a few sketches loose on the desk in her study, but no one commented on them and she resisted the urge to point them out. All in good time.

They were gathered around the giant marble pastry-making table in the kitchen, eating from a box of artisanal chocolates that Lina had picked up in town when Darias's phone rang.

"It's Gibran." He answered. Then frowned.

"You're kidding. He can't do that, can he?" Darias looked right at Beatriz, alarm in his eyes.

Beatriz felt a stab of anxiety pierce her gut. They must be talking about Lorenzo.

16

Darias continued staring at Beatriz—unnerving—as he listened to Gibran. He let out a curse. "We'll see about that. I'll get my lawyer on it today. If he refuses to talk to us, then other people might start to fight back as well. We need the ability to call anyone in for questioning, especially these high-ranking types."

Darias hung up. "Lorenzo's refused the interview. He's lawyered up, and they're saying there's no legal grounds for the interview to take place."

Beatriz hesitated, her loyalty to Lorenzo suddenly fierce. "Well, there isn't, is there? He hasn't done anything. He wasn't anywhere near the murders. He isn't in the Cross of Blood and had nothing to do with Emma's kidnapping or Sandro getting shot. I don't know why Gibran would want to talk to him."

"Because he's trying to find out who's sending you the texts."

"It's not Lorenzo. I'm sure of it."

"Have you ever received one while you're with him?" Darias lifted a brow.

"No, but—" She inhaled. "This person has only texted me on two occasions."

"Both times when you were about to meet Lorenzo. Aren't you the least bit suspicious?"

"No." Her voice rose. "I'm not. And I think it's rotten of you to attack him. I've finally found a man I really like and you all want to come after him like he's a criminal." She felt tears closing her throat. "He doesn't deserve that, and neither do I."

She wanted them all out of her house right now. Especially Darias.

"I wish Rigo were here," said Lina. "He'd know what to do."

Beatriz wanted to observe that the revered and respected Rigo actually liked Lorenzo but no one would believe her right now.

"I've asked him to come repeatedly," said Darias. "He has some case that's more important to him than his own flesh and blood."

"Every case he has is the most important one in the world." Lina sighed. "He's always been like that. I suppose it's why he's such a good lawyer."

"Well, I wish he'd put his talents to work in service of the family for a change."

"He'll come. He promised he'd be here by the summer," said Lina.

"I'm heading back. I have to meet with the vineyard manager. And I'm going to call my lawyer on the way. We can't let him get away with this."

Darias nodded his goodbyes. Emma hesitated. "I'll stay a bit if that's okay," she said softly.

"Sure." He kissed her warmly on the cheek. "I'll be home for dinner."

As the door closed behind him, Emma leaned into Beatriz. "I'm sorry about Darias being so gruff. The responsibility of being king weighs heavily on him."

"I know." Beatriz had managed to get her tears under control. "But sometimes I think he forgets he's my twin brother, not my lord and master. You guys do realize that Lorenzo isn't behind this, don't you?" She looked from her mom to Emma and back.

Her mom stroked her arm. "We're with you one hundred percent, sweetie. I wish he would have just gone ahead with the interview and cleared the air. But it'll blow over. Don't worry. Will you show us what you plan to do with the gardens?"

Beatriz let out a long sigh. She wished she could tell them how much Lorenzo had already done for her. He was the one who'd built her confidence enough for her to even think about renovating this place.

But patience had always been one of her virtues. She was good at quietly waiting. It had been trained into her from an early age. One day they'd all know what a wonderful, warm and giving man Lorenzo was, and until then she'd best keep her mouth shut. "Sure. I've been talking to a landscaper, and they're bringing in some trees for an orchard next week. Let's go."

Beatriz had intended to ride back to the palace with them—she'd left her own car there—but now she wanted to be alone to talk to Lorenzo so she convinced them to leave her behind. She apologized to Nina for the lack of warning—neither of them had an overnight bag—and arranged for her car and some essential items to be brought by the staff.

As soon as she was alone in her bedroom with the door closed, she picked up her phone and called Lorenzo.

"Hello, Beatriz." He spoke softly, but she could hear a hint of reserve in his voice.

"Why did you refuse the interview?" She couldn't hold back.

"As I said before, I'm a businessman with a reputation to protect. I can't allow myself to be called in for questioning when there's no evidence— circumstantial or otherwise—to suggest that I'm guilty of anything."

"But just refusing makes you look guilty." She paced around her room. "They'll think you have something to hide. And most likely you'll have to do it anyway."

"My lawyer assures me that a judge will uphold my right to refuse unless further evidence is produced." His voice shimmered with steel. "And there will be no further evidence because, as we both know, I had nothing to do with the texts or the murders or anything else."

She sighed. "I'm just upset because everything was starting to go well. I was finally ready to introduce you to everyone as my...my boyfriend. Now they're all upset and on edge about this. Well, Darias is, anyway."

"And he's the king."

"Exactly."

"But he's also your brother so I'm sure you can talk sense into him."

"It's precisely because he's my brother that I can't talk sense in to him." She sighed. "He was overprotective before he became king. Now he's impossible."

"Your brother Rigo called me this afternoon."

"What?" She spun around. "Why?"

"I guess Darias told him about the situation. He told me to tread very carefully because at heart this is a murder investigation. He also happened to point out that you told me the location of the Cross of Blood initiation where Sandro was shot."

"What? How did he even know that?" Beatriz blinked, her brain spinning.

"I don't know, but you did tell me the location. That it would be right there, at the lake house."

"So what? You weren't here that night." She glanced around, suddenly spooked.

"But if I was part of some big conspiracy, which they seem to suspect, I could have told others about it."

Did you? Doubts suddenly creaked inside her. She brushed them away. Lorenzo had done nothing whatsoever that was suspicious.

Why had Rigo called Lorenzo instead of her? Her brothers were enough to drive anyone to drink. "What else did Rigo say?"

"That he'd be arriving soon to bring his sharp legal mind to bear on the situation."

She knew those weren't her brother's exact words. He was far too cagey for that. "Well, that's good. He might see something that everyone else has missed. And I wish you'd reconsider and go talk to Gibran. It can be private. No one will even know you did it."

"Impossible. In this day and age everyone knows what everyone did, and if they don't know it now it will come out later. The gossip papers have started printing pictures of you and me together. I'm sure they'd love a story about how the princess's new lover is under suspicion of murder."

"So you think we should stop seeing each other?" Her mind immediately ran to the worst case scenario.

"Rigo made that suggestion."

"What?" Her blood boiled. "Who does he think he is? My brothers are so arrogant to think they can tell me what to do. Except without even bothering to talk to me. You're not going to listen to him, are you?"

"No. It's just important to keep news of our romance entirely separate from stories about the criminal investigation into the conspiracy against your family. And let's postpone my having dinner with them until this blows over. That would just be awkward if they all suspect me of something."

"I suppose you're right." She looked out the window toward the lake. The sun disappeared behind the tall mountains by late afternoon and the whole landscape took on an eerie glamour. She suddenly felt a deep ache of loneliness. "Can you come over?"

"I'm on my way right now."

Relief flooded her veins. At least this wasn't going to come between them. "See you soon."

She put her phone down and stretched to release some of the tension tightening her muscles. Then her phone pinged again. She picked it up, half hoping he'd sent her a reassuring romantic message.

But it was from another unknown number. Heart pumping, she pressed the button.

What makes you so sure Lorenzo isn't the murderer?

Her flesh prickled, and she glanced over her shoulder. She wanted to text something back. *I just know.* But she didn't. She didn't want to engage with whoever this creep was.

At least she knew for sure it wasn't Lorenzo. He'd hardly send a text suggesting his own guilt.

I should tell Nina. She didn't want to. It would unleash a firestorm of new drama. Gibran would rush

over here and guards would man the perimeter and—
if the last two times were any guide—nothing else
would happen. These texts could be from some
random person hundreds or thousands of miles away
who just wanted to mess with her.

And she wanted to be alone with Lorenzo, to heal
the wounds caused by this legal mess and shore up
their relationship before some other missile was
lobbed at it.

She held her phone, debating what to do. She
decided to sit tight until Lorenzo arrived. At least
then if they did report it they could present a united
front.

*Another text arrived when you were about to meet
Lorenzo?* She could hear the suspicious murmurs
already. Even if she did tell them, what could they do
that they weren't doing already?

But she might go out of her mind worrying and
waiting. And what if he was in danger? She dialed
Lorenzo's number.

He picked up. "I'm at the gate. Nina's opening it
for me."

"Thank goodness."

"Is anything wrong?" Concern deepened his voice.

"I'll tell you in a minute."

She rushed downstairs to meet him at the front
door, then hesitated before opening it, peering
through the peephole. The afternoon had faded into
dusk and long shadows from the mountains hovered
over the landscape and the house. She watched the
glow of his headlights crawl up the drive and stop
near the door.

Once he was climbing the steps, she opened the
door. "What's going on?" His jaw was taut.

"Something's wrong, isn't it?"

Beatriz glanced over his shoulder to where Nina was climbing out of her car. "I'll tell you upstairs."

His brow furrowed, but he followed her up. In her bedroom she closed the door, picked up her phone and showed him the text.

He stared at it. "You think it's me?" She was surprised to hear anger in his voice.

"Of course not! Why would you send a text accusing yourself? And I wouldn't show it to you if I thought it was you. But I didn't want to tell Nina and bring the whole palace security apparatus down on our heads. They'd just press harder to interrogate you."

"My lawyer assures me that is impossible."

"Unless there's another incident. And whoever is behind this could make that happen." She shivered involuntarily.

Lorenzo gathered her into his arms. She realized they hadn't even kissed yet, both so tense and overwrought from the events of the day. "Relax. Don't worry. I won't let anything happen to you."

"I know." She sank into his strength. "I'm just worn out after all the drama today. I brought my family here to show them the house, though. They loved it. They don't think I'm crazy for fixing it up anymore."

"They thought you were crazy?"

"Yes." She let a smile pull at her mouth. "It's been uninhabited and used only as a place for macho hunting parties since the 1960s at least. And then the murders…" She drew in a ragged breath. "But I told them I feel close to Dad and Grandmama here. That I've taken the house back for us."

Lorenzo kissed her softly on the lips. "You've brought it to life again."

"I should give you credit for having the vision. I didn't really think of it until you started talking about this place."

"It's my business to spot potential in neglected real estate." He kissed her softly again. "And even perhaps in people."

"Like me?" Her eyes opened.

"Like you." He nuzzled her gently, the stubble of his face tickling her skin. "I know you're a princess, but I had a hunch you were still in tight bud form and needed some encouragement to open up and blossom in all your glory."

Beatriz giggled. Joy unfurled in her chest at how apt his image was. "It seems you were right. At least I've started the unfurling process."

"You're well on your way to full bloom." A warm grin spread across his face. "And I'm enjoying every glorious minute of it. Has Signora Pazzi's team started on your new designs yet?"

"They're almost done. She's hired a model for next Tuesday so I can see them in action. Would you like to come?"

"I'd love it." He laid a warm kiss on her lips. "I can't wait until all of Milan—all of the fashion world—can see what my beautiful Beatriz is capable of."

A twinge of nerves tightened her stomach. "What if they hate my designs?"

"Impossible." He lifted a brow. "Remember how I told you I can spot potential?"

"Yes," she said slowly.

"I see the potential for a very successful fashion

brand in your designs. You have an eye for what flatters a woman."

"I think you're the expert in flattery," she teased.

"It's not flattery if it's the honest truth." He lowered his arms to around her waist. "Are you hungry?"

"Not really. We had a big lunch in town."

"Me too. I vote that we skip dinner and head right to bed." Mischief danced in his gray eyes.

"We are conveniently located to do that," she said primly, fighting a smile.

He'd already started to peel off her black sweater, lifting it up over her head and exposing her bra. Her fingers reached for his belt. It was easy to forget all the chaos outside when she was alone with Lorenzo. He made her feel complete.

She slid his pants down his legs, and he stepped out of them. "Lie down on the bed," she commanded softly.

She looked up to see a slight smile cross his face. "Yes, your majesty."

He spread his magnificent body across the white bedcovers. Muscled and tanned, he looked good enough to eat. She shrugged out of her clothes and climbed over him and began to kiss him all over.

She let her tongue explore the hollows between his muscles, and her lips trail over the hard ridges. The scent of him, warm and musky and all male, sent her senses into overdrive. Finally she took him in her mouth and sucked, feeling a thrill at giving him pleasure. Who'd have thought that quiet, bookish Beatriz would find herself in bed with such an exciting man?

Her sense of power and joy grew along with his

obvious arousal. When a thick groan escaped him, she slid her tongue along his length, then climbed on top of him, taking him inside her. She'd quietly gone on contraception so they no longer had to worry about condoms.

She eased herself slowly down on top of him, feeling him inside her, filling her. His eyes were closed, and his handsome face relaxed in a blissful expression. She loved that he encouraged her to take charge—not just of their bodies but her life. She rode him, tentatively at first, then with passion and excitement as sensations and emotions rose inside her.

She'd never dreamed she'd be lucky enough to meet a man like Lorenzo: brilliant, handsome and confident. On the fairly frequent occasions she'd been fixed up with someone, it was always a dull blue blood whose only claim to fame or success was his family connections. Those brief relationships had been stilted and disappointing. And now—all by herself—she'd found a man that any woman would be excited to call her own.

My own. Lorenzo had stuck by her through all the family drama. He held his head high through all the suspicion and doubt and name calling because he knew— as she did—that he was above all that.

His hands roamed up and down her arms as he writhed with pleasure beneath her, until suddenly he gripped and she felt his climax rip through them both with volcanic force. Her own climax followed, and she felt her inner muscles grip him as explosive waves of sensation shook her.

She collapsed onto his chest, panting, and he wrapped his arms tightly around her. "My Beatriz. My beautiful Beatriz." His words caused a further shudder deep inside her, in her heart as well as lower.

I love you.

She wanted to say it but caught herself at the last moment. Her upbringing had taught her to be cautious and guarded. She'd learned early on to expect people to try to take advantage of her because she was royal and wealthy, and even now, in the arms of her lover, those same warnings flashed somewhere deep in her brain.

He had to say it first.

But would he?

17

The next day Lorenzo left early to catch a flight and she debated whether to tell Gibran, or even Nina, about the text. She decided not to.

"Everything okay?" asked Nina when she came down to breakfast.

"Great." She pushed a confident smile to her lips. This was her time to build her dream, and she wasn't going to be distracted or derailed by family drama or outside interference.

There were only two weeks left before the show. All the clothes needed to be finished and the models styled. She'd sent out rather mysterious invitations without her name on them and contacted agencies to secure models, but as a new, unnamed designer, the response hadn't been great and there was still a lot to do to make the show a success. It was a huge undertaking, and since she was determined to keep the whole endeavor secret as long as possible, she'd be doing much of it herself—with help from Lorenzo and his list of experienced contacts.

And she'd applied to the fashion institute in Milan. She didn't tell a soul—even Lorenzo, who thought it was a waste of time for someone in her position. She craved the in-depth knowledge of materials, techniques and fashion history she could acquire only from being a true student. She wanted to be able to cut and sew like Signora Pazzi, even if she then hired someone else to do it. Otherwise she knew she'd always feel like an imposter, a princess playing the role of fashion designer as a hobby.

She made breakfast under Nina's watchful eye. "I'm going to ride my horse at ten, then head out to Milan." She was visiting a modeling agency that afternoon to choose some models for the show. Competition for top models was stiff during fashion week.

"As usual." Nina smiled.

"It must get boring for you. I'm sorry. Do you want some coffee?"

"No, thanks, and I'm not bored. This is my job. As long as you're safe, I'm happy."

Beatriz felt a twinge of guilt for not telling her about the text from last night, but really, what good would it do?

"Does anyone ever ask you where I go all day?"

"I have to file a report of my activities—and by extension your activities—with Gibran. Other than that no one has asked me anything."

"I suppose we've all become used to having a security detail."

"It's probably easy when you're used to having servants around all the time."

"I suppose so." Beatriz sipped her coffee. "But we don't call them servants anymore. We prefer the term *staff*." Nina stared at her. "Though maybe no one cares except us. Regardless, I appreciate your discretion. I haven't told my family the reason why I'm spending so much time in Milan." Maybe it was time to confide in Nina. Everyone would know sooner or later. "I'm putting together a collection of clothes for Milan fashion week. Please don't tell anyone, okay!"

"I won't. I'll keep your secrets." Nina looked pleased to be privy to this privileged information. "But won't they find out sooner or later?"

"All in good time."

The collection was for the following fall and winter, and Beatriz had distilled her ideas down to a single clear theme of sleek black and silver essentials and accessories with simple, clean lines and inventive textures.

She and Lorenzo had consulted with an event planner over the show itself and were assured that the affair would be as elegant as her collection. The guest list was more challenging and had involved a lot of late nights looking up the names of important fashion journalists and influential buyers.

"Anna Wintour? Is she really going to come?" Beatriz had looked down the sofa toward Lorenzo, who was giving her a foot massage.

"Only if you invite her." He kissed her foot. "You know what I always say…"

"Aim high."

"Exactly."

She shivered at the sensation of his lips on the arch of her foot. "I'd never dare do any of this if it wasn't for you."

"Then I'm glad to be here. I'd be glad to be here even if I wasn't encouraging and supporting a talented designer about to make her debut, but that does add some sparkle to the experience."

A talented designer. All her life she'd been the dull one. The bluestocking princess who coasted through life on her famous name and her family fortune. She'd never stunned anyone with her talent, and despite being reputedly "bookish" she wasn't actually academic. She just loved to read books and no one paid you money or gave you awards for that, did they?

But now she—with the help of Lorenzo—had found something she was actually good at. Signora Pazzi loved her designs and said they were surprisingly easy to cut and sew because they moved so naturally with the body. The models who came to the atelier had oohed and ahhed over how comfortable they were. This late in the game it would be tricky to secure any top models for the show, but the agency said that if they revealed her real identity— which would have to happen sooner or later—they'd have their pick.

One night, after a long day in Milan, she drew in a breath, nerves spiking. "Do you think it's time for me to come out of the closet?"

"You're a lesbian?" He lifted a brow.

"Only in your kinky fantasies." She kicked him gently with the foot he'd been massaging. "I mean...do you think it's time to connect my name to the show?"

"Yes. Absolutely." He'd been lounging on the sofa, but he sat up. "I've been longing for you to be ready to bask in the spotlight."

"I'm nervous." The idea terrified her. "And I'd have to tell my family first. What if they're horrified and want me to cancel?"

"It's far too late for that. The show is less than two

weeks away. And if you come out now it'll bring in some top names who still have your invitation in their stack of 'maybes.' "

"It could get me some big-name models too."

"That's great for getting publicity." Lorenzo looked ready to spring into action. "Shall we put together a press release? I can have my assistants distribute it as soon as you've broken the news to your family."

"A press release. Goodness, that sounds so…official."

"It is official, my love. It's happening. You've created a stunning collection, and you're going to be the hottest show in town. I think you should put your name on it as soon as possible."

Excitement mingled with nerves. The prospect of actually being respected, maybe even admired, for something that she'd done warred with the loss of the privacy she cherished. "What if people want to interview me? I'd be so nervous."

"You can tell them there will be no interviews until after the show. That'll heighten the sense of mystery. They'll be ten deep in the standing room."

Beatriz drew in a breath. "Okay. Let's do it."

The next day at dinner, she sat at the table with her mom, Darias and Emma, also Sandro and Serena, who were in town to make arrangements for their upcoming wedding. Thank goodness Aunt Liesel had finally gone home. Her only regret was that Lorenzo wasn't by her side. He'd held firm about not talking to Gibran or anyone else involved in the criminal investigation, and a local judge had upheld his right to refuse an interview. Those inside the palace who knew of his refusal still took a very dim view of it.

But Beatriz knew they'd change their minds about him once they knew how much he'd done to support her in pursuing her dream.

"What's going on?" Lina passed a plate of tiny appetizers that the chef had prepared as samples for the wedding. Beatriz took a salmon puff pastry. "You said you had something to tell us."

"Please God don't let it be that you've eloped with Lorenzo Aldobrando," said Darias, passing the hors d'oeuvres to Serena.

"Darias! Don't be so mean." Lina scolded him. "Beatriz is entitled to do what ever she wants. She's a grown woman."

"Thank you, Mama." Her mom's warm support of her never wavered. If she ever became a mom she wanted to be just like her. Darias's cold remark did, however, remind her of the kind of thing she might have said in his place. She'd been suspicious of his instant bride, especially after she found the contract between them—outlining their obligations to each other for the term of one year.

"Well, have you?" Darias took a bite of a sausage pastry.

"It's nothing to do with Lorenzo." She sucked in a breath, heart pounding. Was she really going to tell them? "Well, not really. I'm designing a line of clothing."

Silence.

"That's wonderful," said Lina. "For you to wear? Is Alphonse making them?"

Great. Her mom assumed she was designing her own summer wardrobe, like a true little princess. "Actually it's for anyone to buy. I'm planning a show for fashion week in Milan."

"But that's this month," said Sandro with an amused smile. "Serena and I are planning to go to Armani and Dolce & Gabbana."

She looked around the table. No one thought she was serious. She straightened her shoulders and forged ahead. "My show is on the twenty-ninth. It's a collection of fall and winter wear, and I'd love for you all to come."

"Did Lorenzo put you up to this?" asked Darias.

Beatriz resisted the urge to throw something at him. "It's something I've dreamed of since I was little. I've always designed clothes, I just didn't show them to anyone. He encouraged me to get one of my designs made, and it all built from there." She spoke fast and grew louder as she went. "The entire collection is in the final stages at an atelier in Milan, and the venue for the show is booked and it's happening."

She looked around. More silence, this time the stunned-into-silence variety. "What? You can't believe I'm capable of it? You think it's going to be a disaster?"

"No, sweetheart, of course not." Her mom's usually smooth brow was furrowed. "But you know how hard the media can be on us."

"Is that all you can think of? No one's even interested in seeing my designs?" She pulled her phone from her pocket. "I have some right here, which I'd show you if anyone cared. Which I guess you don't. At least Lorenzo is supportive."

She felt Darias bristle.

"Well, it's true. Dad laughed at me when I said I wanted to study fashion. None of you were supportive, either. If I'd told any of you about my plans for this show, you would have talked me out of it, like you're almost trying to do now, except that it's too late because the show is going ahead. The press releases are ready to go out, and I just wanted to let you know before it goes public."

"You could use a brand name, you know," offered Sandro. "So no one knows it's you."

"That's what I intended to do, but now that it's here I'm proud of my collection and I want people to know I made it. Why shouldn't I get to put my name on my own work? People think it's so great being a princess, but really it's just an excuse for people to ignore everything about you except that you're a princess."

"And being a princess will be great publicity for your show," said Serena. "It'll get you more attention."

"Of the wrong kind," muttered Darias.

"Not necessarily," said Serena. "And sometimes even the wrong kind of attention can have the right results. All the drama over my surprise pregnancy and sudden royal engagement blew up into a big book deal." Serena was a blogger who had lived her life in the public eye even before she'd met Sandro. "My channel has never been more popular, and I'm getting opportunities that wouldn't have come my way before."

Sandro had walked around the table and now wrapped his arms around Beatriz. "I think it's wonderful, Bea. You've always been an artist. I bet the show is going to be fabulous. Can I see your photos?"

Once she started passing her phone around and

they could see she was not only serious but talented and accomplished, their attitude changed. Her mom got tears in her eyes and kissed her. "You have to promise me I can buy that leather coat, okay?"

"Okay, Mama." Beatriz found herself getting choked up.

"And I want the feather stole," said Serena. "And those black pants with the silver pinstripe. I was just on a New York late-night show and that would have been amazing to wear. I might get invited again closer to the wedding."

"Serena gets great publicity," said Sandro proudly. "They never want to say anything bad about her."

"I think it's my Cinderella story," she said with a chuckle. "And who wants to be mean to a pregnant lady?" Sandro and Serena's baby was due at the end of September.

"That's true," said Lina with a smile. "They wait until afterward when you can't lose the weight fast enough. But since you still look perfect you won't have that problem."

"Did that really happen?" asked Beatriz.

"Oh, yes." Lina grinned. "Every time. My only comeback was to get pregnant again as soon as possible."

"How do you still look so fabulous after having five sets of twins?" Serena looked genuinely curious.

Lina leaned toward her. "Don't tell anyone, but I had a tummy tuck five years ago." She winked. "I think they removed about a yard of extra skin."

"Mama! Stop it." Beatriz was appalled but also laughing. "You didn't!"

"I did." Lina sipped her wine. "You'd never know, either. The surgeon was very skilled. Not that anyone will ever see me naked again anyway."

"Nonsense. You'll be ready to date sooner or later," said Sandro. "You're far too young to lock yourself in a cloister."

"I'm just fine in my cloister, thank you very much. Let's get back to the topic at hand. My brilliant and beautiful daughter Beatriz and her upcoming show. We need champagne!"

"I'm a little nervous," Beatriz admitted. "The press releases are going out tomorrow, and the whole world will know."

Her mom leaned over from her chair to hug her. "All the more reason to celebrate."

18

Lorenzo's office sent out the press releases the following morning to journalists and fashion buyers all over the world. He'd arranged for his assistant to handle the RSVPs and pass along the list to the event planners managing the event. Coverage popped up first in the fashion press, with headlines like "Princess Beatriz of Altaleone Announces a Line of Ready-to-Wear." Word spread to the celebrity gossip sites, where the headlines morphed into "Designing Princess" and "Royal Designs on the Runway." They'd included a chic publicity photo of her dressed in one of her own black jackets, and the image appeared over and over again.

"So far so good," said Lorenzo by phone that night. He was in Rome on business. "All the publicity is positive."

"I know. Nothing about you and me." She'd been nervous about stories trying to make a scandal out of their relationship, but no one had even mentioned it. It made her a little sad.

"I'm not important enough or wrong enough for them to build a story out of," Lorenzo said ruefully. "Now if they knew I was wanted for questioning by the palace, they'd have a story."

"I see your point. Luckily no one's talking about that anymore. And the family were so happy about my show—once they got over their shock, that is. I think we should reschedule that dinner. I really want you to all get to know one another." She didn't want awkwardness at the show. She wanted to proudly show Lorenzo off as her boyfriend and have him seem like part of the family. The media would be there in force and watching all of them.

"I'd like that too."

"I'll talk to my mom tomorrow about when we can all meet." Her heart swelled. Lorenzo was so patient with her ridiculous family situation. How many men would put up with such nonsense?

Any man would jump at the chance to marry a princess.

One of Liesel's annoying mutterings popped into her head. Liesel managed to haunt one with her phobias and warnings, even when she was miles away in Germany.

Still, Lorenzo hadn't actually said he loved her.

She hadn't said it either. But she felt it in her heart and her mind more and more every day. She trusted him to manage the press release and invitations—sure he had her best interests at heart. But why didn't she dare to reveal her true feelings? Was she still worried that he was only dating her because of her royal connections or—worse—because he still harbored a secret hope of getting his hands on the lake property?

"Would you still be interested in me if I wasn't a princess?" She asked it boldly but with a teasing tone in her voice.

"Of course I would. Life would be easier if you weren't a princess. We wouldn't have to be tailed everywhere by security and worry about press stories every time we're out together."

She bit her lip. Maybe instead of being a draw for Lorenzo, as she'd assumed, her royal status was a big negative. Everyone knew that being a princess was a job for life. She could never go anywhere incognito or decide to live under the radar. Everything she did—everyone she associated with—would always be fodder for the press and subject to idle speculation.

"But I don't mind those things. You're more than worth it. I wish I was there with you right now."

"Me too." She lay back on her bed, visualizing his features. She needed to be patient. They were falling in love with each other. It wasn't one sided. In time he'd voice the feelings she longed to hear—and in the meantime she'd have her show to keep her busy.

The two weeks before the show raced by. Beatriz's garments were ready except for final on-model adjustments. After the initial flurry there were no further articles about her or her designs—or her and Lorenzo. And the long-anticipated and dreaded dinner with the family took place at the palace and was smooth and cordial. Everything was going swimmingly.

So why did she still have a knot in the pit of her stomach?

She told herself it was just nerves about doing something so new. She'd never put herself out in public for anything beyond routine royal events before and certainly never deliberately drawn the spotlight to herself.

And her romance with Lorenzo, wonderful as it was, made her more emotional. She found herself swinging readily from joy to worried tears, especially when he wasn't there to hold her hand and tell her everything would be okay.

On the day of the show she ran around like a crazy person, checking the models' makeup and hair and making last-minute tweaks to the clothes. The catered food for the after-party got stuck in fashion week traffic and arrived late and people were RSVP-ing yes right up until the last second, complicating the guest list and the seating arrangements.

Her family sat in the front row, next to editors from *Vogue*, *L'Officiel*, *W* and *Elle*. Her mom and garrulous brothers chatted easily with journalists and celebrities, and Emma helped Serena livestream vlog the buildup to the show to her audience of devoted followers.

Lorenzo hovered backstage with her. The music came on when it was supposed to. The models marched confidently, swung and swayed and swaggered as they showed off her clothes. Her eyes zeroed in on tiny imperfections—a half-buttoned button, the sticker on the bottom of a boot—but as each look came out and was greeted by applause and murmurs of approval from the crowd, her anxiety turned to exhilaration.

After the last model had walked, Lorenzo pushed her out to join them for the finale. They'd agreed that she would say a few words, and although the prospect terrified her, she knew it was better to speak for herself rather than have the press put words in her mouth.

She had a portable mic in her hand, and the first two times she tried to speak, her voice disappeared into the roar of applause. Finally, the crowd hushed enough for her to try again. Heart thudding, she prayed she wouldn't burst into tears. "Thank you for coming." She could see famous faces out there. "I'm sure you were all surprised to hear that I had designed a fashion line, and I want to assure you that it is my own work, not simply something that I put my name to."

She spoke proudly, since their appreciation of her work had been obvious. "I do want to thank a very good friend of mine"—she turned toward the backstage area—"who encouraged and supported me every step of the way and whose confidence in me often outstripped my own, Lorenzo Aldobrando." Lorenzo stepped forward, looking only at her. Then he took her hand and lifted it high in the air—as designers often did with their models at a fashion show finale—and they exited together.

Backstage, out of the view of the cameras, he kissed her full and hard on the mouth. Her heart was full to bursting.

"You did it," he murmured, holding both her hands. "It was magnificent."

"I did it." She could hardly believe it. "Thanks to you. I quite literally couldn't have done it without you."

He shook his head and huffed a denial. "I offered barely more than lip service. I'm just glad all that talent of yours isn't buried deep inside the palace anymore. You deserve the spotlight." He placed a soft kiss on her lips. "You'd better go out there and mingle with your fans."

"Do I have to? Can't we just go back to the lake house and celebrate in private?" she whispered.

"Soon." A smile played about his sensual mouth. "But first, duty calls."

Journalists were already finding their way backstage so she gave some informal interviews and enjoyed a lot of congratulations. Her mom was teary-eyed with pride, and Sandro and Darias were both rude enough to say how surprised they were.

"You didn't think your sister had it in her?" She arched an imperious brow, laughing inwardly.

"I feel terrible for laughing along with Dad when you suggested studying fashion years ago," said Darias. "I'm so glad you ignored us idiots and did it anyway."

"The credit for that goes to Lorenzo," she said proudly. This would cement their newly forming positive view of him. "It was all his idea. After I told him how much I loved fashion, of course."

Darias slapped Lorenzo on the back in a brotherly fashion. She got sucked into a conversation with a buyer from a New York department store, but she could see Lorenzo chatting with Sandro and Darias as if they were great friends and that made her almost as happy as the success of the show.

Afterward they all went out to dinner and had a lovely time talking about her experience designing and making the clothes, choosing the fabrics and dealing with the quirky but brilliant Signora Pazzi. Then she and Lorenzo drove back to the lake house and made love until they were both wrung out and exhausted.

Lorenzo had to leave early the next morning to catch a flight to New York for a meeting about some real estate he was buying there, and she was quite happy to be left alone to bask in the afterglow of her first show.

Around nine-thirty she grabbed a quick coffee, then headed for the palace to ride her horse, with

Nina in hot pursuit as usual. She'd asked the palace clipping service to pull any articles about her show, and she couldn't resist ducking into her mom's office to peek at the stack of articles from that morning's papers and any prominent website features.

On top was an effusive article from the tiny local paper, which praised her talents and beauty and the royal Leone family and was mostly just embarrassing.

The next one was totally different. It was an article clipped from a Milan paper known for insightful coverage of the fashion industry. The headline, "Wealthy Princess Buys Herself a Place in the Fashion Week Calendar," made her heart seize. Well, she kind of had done that, hadn't she? Biting her lip, she started to read the article. By the time she got to the words "dry, derivative and reminiscent of first-year fashion school efforts," her hands were shaking too much for her to read on.

It's just one person's opinion.

She grabbed the next article, from a Paris paper: "Princess Beatriz of Altaleone proves money can't buy talent." *What?*

Tears threatening, she snatched at the next one: "Princess parades a line that looks like it came off the rack at Monoprix."

Frantic, she shuffled through them. Nearly all slammed her clothes as dull and uninventive. Some called her the "plain princess" or asked, "Did you ever hear of Princess Beatriz of Altaleone before? Us neither…" before enumerating reasons why she should stick to garden parties.

Tears blurred her vision, and an audible sob rose in her throat. How? They'd all seemed so pleased! Was it fake? Or a joke on her that everyone else got and she missed?

She pulled out her phone and pressed Lorenzo's number with a trembling finger. But she got his voice mail. He must be on board his trans-Atlantic flight.

There were articles about her and Lorenzo too. She locked the office door and barricaded herself in while she read them. "Notorious real estate investor Lorenzo Aldobrando is involved in a new speculation—on the heart and hand of a princess." One article included pictures of him with several beautiful women, "none of them as wealthy as his new blue-blooded conquest."

She went through them all, scanning and reading, hoping and praying for at least one positive perspective to buoy her wrecked confidence. Apart from that first article, by a paper she knew from experience to be a purveyor of local fluff, they were all somewhere between dismissive and savage.

Had her mom seen these? Her mom's personal secretary had brought them here, and she might well have browsed through them. Otherwise, Beatriz would be tempted to burn them in the fireplace.

A knock on the door made her jump. "Beatriz?" Her mom's voice. The handle turned, but the door was locked so it didn't open.

"I'm in here." She swiped at her tear-stained cheeks with her sleeve. "Hold on." She opened the door, heart somewhere down around her belt.

"What's the matter?" Her mom's zeroed in on the papers in her hand.

"Nothing new. Just a Leone family member getting attacked in the press for being privileged and royal." She tried to sound cool and casual about it. Which she should be. This kind of treatment was the norm. Not many people loved you for being born into wealth and power beyond most people's imaginings.

"They're saying mean things about your show?" Her mom looked poleaxed.

"Yep. Boring, dreary, quiet. All the things I usually hear about myself." She was impressed with herself for sounding so hardened.

"But it wasn't boring at all! It was stunning. How could they say that iridescent black feather jacket was dull? They're mad." Her mom was already moving toward her, arms open for a hug. Beatriz sank into her embrace.

"And they wrote poisonous things about Lorenzo." A sob escaped her throat. "Saying that I'm just his latest investment, as if he cares about nothing but the fact that I'm princess."

"Oh, goodness." Her mom stroked her hair. "Where is Lorenzo?"

"On his way to New York for a meeting."

"Already? He does travel a lot, doesn't he?"

"He has real estate holdings all over the world." Beatriz found herself making excuses for him. Why did he have to leave before the crack of dawn on the morning after her big show? Couldn't he have taken one lousy day off to celebrate with her?

Maybe she wasn't as important to him as she thought.

"I'm sure he'll rush back when he finds out about this."

Would he? He hadn't canceled any meetings for her before. Not that she knew of. He was always jetting off somewhere. In a way it was refreshing that he had a life and wasn't trying too hard to suck up to her. His personal success had reassured her wasn't interested in her as a lavish meal ticket.

"I don't know." Her voice was flat. "I was so happy with the show, and I thought it went so well, and now this. Maybe I've been wrong all along about Lorenzo too."

"Oh, darling, don't think like that. I'm sure everything will be fine. You know how the press are."

"I do." She drew in a deep breath and tried to gather strength from her mom. "I guess I just thought it would be different this time."

"Is that Beatriz's car outside?" She heard Sandro's voice from the hallway. "I just heard a story on the radio that Lorenzo Aldobrando applied for development rights on her lake."

19

Beatriz blinked. How could he apply to do anything with land that wasn't even his? Was he so sure he'd be able to talk her into anything? Or was he planning to propose to her so that under Altaleone law he—as the male in the union—would have ultimate rights over her property?

Sandro appeared in the doorway. "Oh, there you are, sis. Did you hear what I said?"

"I heard it." She could barely raise a sound.

"I'm sure it's just some misunderstanding," said her mom bravely. "Who wants a cup of tea?"

"I need to ride Gatto." Right now she just wanted to get away from everyone. And riding would get her nerves and emotions back under control and give her time to think this through.

"Don't take it personally, Bea." Sandro put his arm around her. "The press are a bunch of douchebags. You know that, right?"

"Yep." She attempted a smile. It failed. Sandro must have seen some of the scathing press about her show. She didn't dare ask about what kind of feedback Serena had received for the images from the collection she'd shown on her popular video channel. "I'm fine. Really."

She walked mechanically to the stables, taking care not to catch anyone's eye on the way. Nina, who had been waiting outside the room the whole time, followed behind her like a shadow, as usual. It had gotten to the point that she sometimes forgot Nina was even there.

Beatriz groomed her horse—who was always spotless anyway, thanks to Matteo—and tacked him up herself. Before she mounted she texted Lorenzo and asked him to call her when he landed.

She wondered if he would. Maybe he had more important deals to take care of first.

Her heart constricted at the thought that everything they'd shared might just be fake. She couldn't quite believe it. No. She didn't believe it. Still, right now she didn't know what to think.

After her ride, Beatriz drove back to her house. She craved the solitude of the lake setting. The palace always had way too many people milling about. And if the mystery texter wanted to sneak in and slit her throat, then heck, maybe that would just be an easy way out.

Her phone rang as she was pulling into the driveway. Her heart skipped a beat when she saw it was Lorenzo calling. "Hi," she answered coolly.

"Hello, Bea. What's up?"

She frowned. Why was he talking to her like one of her brothers. "What do you mean what's up? Have you seen the press?"

"I've been on a flight and busy reading through a three-hundred-page contract. More kudos for your show?"

"Quite the reverse. It's been panned around the

globe, and the show only happened yesterday. Sometimes I wish I lived in the days when news could only travel by horse-drawn carriage."

There was a pause. "Panned? What do you mean?" He sounded deadly serious.

He obviously hadn't seen any of the articles. She reached into the back seat for the folder of vitriolic drivel she'd brought with her to either cry over or burn in the grate of one of the magnificent fireplaces. "Here's what someone on the *OK Magazine* website had to say. 'The oldest and least distinguished member of the royal Leone family is rankling at her brother being king and made a desperate effort to distinguish herself with one of the most trite and pointless excuses for fashion seen on the Milan runways in years.' "

"What? I don't believe it."

"You don't? Do you want me to send you the link?" His incredulity was starting to annoy her. She'd warned him that she was scared of bad press before they'd even started this whole thing.

"No, no. I do believe you, I'm just astonished at the reaction. They all seemed really excited about the show."

"Well, I guess they're just a bunch of two-faced kiss-ups until my back is turned." She slammed her car door and strode toward the house.

"But remember, this is just the press. It's not the buyers writing these pieces."

"Who would want to buy my trite and pointless clothes after this?"

"Come on, who actually reads these papers?"

"And websites."

"The glossy magazines have a long run-up to print.

Commentary in *Vogue* or *L'Officiel* and other genuinely influential publications won't be out for months."

"If they even bother now." She walked into the house and threw the folder of poisonous articles down on the hall table.

"Damn. I wish I was there."

"Me too," she said a little too forcefully.

"I could catch the next flight back." There was an edge to his voice.

"What would be the point of that? It won't change anything." She didn't want him to know how much she craved the reassurance of his arms around her. Maybe he was just worried about his investment in her. All his time and hard work cultivating her—and his efforts might go to waste if he didn't rush back now. "I'll be fine. But when are you coming back?"

"I'm supposed to be here for two nights. Meetings all day tomorrow, then I'm taking the red-eye back the day after. I can cancel them. Tell them I have a family emergency."

Her heart squeezed. Would he really do that for her? "No, really, I'm okay. I'd love to see you as soon as you get back, though."

"I'm flying into Zurich. I was going to visit my sister but instead I'll drive right to your house."

"I appreciate it. Good luck with your meeting." He never shared details of his various real estate deals. Not that she ever asked. It wasn't really her business and she didn't want to pry. And she didn't have the strength to ask about his permit request for the lakefront. She just wanted him back. She craved the comfort of his arms more than anything right now.

"Thanks. I'm not expecting any difficulties. Call me any time you need to. You know I'll always make time for you."

She swallowed. "I know. I'd better let you go. I'll talk to you later."

"Is everything okay?" Nina's voice jarred her out of a frozen stance. Once again she'd forgotten Nina was there, just one room away.

"Fine. I'm going to have a hot bath." Maybe that would soothe the tension building inside her. "If anyone calls just take a message."

"I'd be happy to."

Beatriz stomped upstairs reflecting that she really shouldn't ask a private contractor's security staff to take household messages for her and that maybe she was just a spoiled, bratty princess after all.

The weather had warmed up and spring flowers were blooming everywhere so it was hard to get excited about lighting the gas fire in the bedroom grate, but she did it anyway. As water filled the huge stone tub in her beautiful bathroom, she crumpled up each article and threw them into the flames. Chemicals in the ink and paper threw out colorful flames.

When the cruel articles—and the one lame positive one—were all gone she didn't feel satisfied, so she snatched up the drawings on her desk—ideas for her spring collection. Pain stabbed her at the memory of the joy she'd felt while drawing them. Pretty white dresses that had seemed both demure and sexy at the same time now looked…trite and pointless.

What had she been thinking? She'd let her tiara go to her head, as Aunt Liesel had once accused her of doing when she threw a childish tantrum decades ago. She crumpled the drawings—no easy feat since they were on quality paper—and shoved them into the flames as well.

Destroying her creations didn't even give her a momentary sense of satisfaction. Instead it gave her an ugly feeling that she'd let the bastards win. That the happiness she'd enjoyed over the past few weeks was going to be taken from her—all of it—leaving her alone and sad in her newly renovated palatial residence. Poor little Princess Beatriz…

Cry me a freaking river.

Beatriz managed to lose herself in a gory and engrossing psychological thriller, and it was almost dark when she finally went down to the kitchen to forage for dinner. She spread some goat cheese on a slice of bread and poured honey over it and was about to disappear back to her bedroom when Nina emerged from her suite near the kitchen. "I thought you might want to see this."

Nina held out her phone. Beatriz frowned. She didn't want to see anything except her pillow, preferably for days. But she didn't want to be rude so she took the phone and groaned inwardly when she saw it was an article on the website of the local paper. The letters were tiny, and she had to enlarge them to read, "Princess's Beau Called in for Questioning."

Her plate wobbled in her hand, and she put it down on the marble counter. The article detailed how Lorenzo had been summoned to meet with the palace security staff but had refused and his lawyer had managed to get a judge to agree that the request was unconstitutional.

"How did they get this information?" she murmured aloud.

"I don't know," said Nina. "I just thought you'd

want—"

"I don't want to see any more articles from any publications or websites." She thrust Nina's phone back. "In future please keep them to yourself."

"I'm sorry, I thought you—"

"Please don't make any assumptions about my thoughts." She grabbed her plate and swept imperiously from the room, regretting her rudeness as she mounted the stairs. Nina just wanted to keep her informed. Still, she'd had it up to here and if she couldn't get away from the media circus in her own remote house, then where could she?

Lorenzo called as she was getting ready for bed. "Hi, beautiful. I miss you. How are you doing?"

She climbed onto her bed and relaxed back into the pillows, enjoying sweet relief at the sound of his voice. "I'm hanging in there. How are you?"

"How did the local rag find out that your security staff wanted to question me?"

Suddenly she felt tired. Very tired. "I burned all my drawings."

"What?"

"Not that you care. Maybe the press is right and you only want access to my land and wealth." A rogue urge to shatter everything surged inside her.

There was a long silence. "Do you really believe that?"

"I don't know what to believe anymore."

"Beatriz." She heard a growl. "I'm so angry with myself for not being there with you right now. I should have listened to my gut instincts this morning and jumped on a plane back. But listen, the show is going over well with buyers. Have you checked the email account we set up?"

She had to think for a moment to figure out what he was talking about. His assistant had set up an account linked to a branded website for interested people to get in touch. It hadn't crossed her mind to look at it, mostly because his assistant had handled all the details so far. "No. I'm a princess and just sit around reading novels all day," she said truthfully.

"I wish I could shake you. Go there and read the emails right now."

"Hang on." She put her phone down and brought her laptop to her bed, then punched up the email account. Her eye scanned the list of senders. "I don't recognize any of those names."

"Buyers are not generally household names. But look, Jill Kinsky from Barneys sent you two emails, one about buys she wants to make for this collection and another asking to discuss the next season."

Beatriz frowned and pulled up the email. "Barneys is in New York, right?"

"Yes, very chichi department store. Sets the trends for other high-end retail. And she *loved* your collection."

"Damn." Beatriz blinked.

"And scroll down, there's one from Leah MacDonald at Nordstrom. She's interested in making a big buy for their fall season."

"Nordstrom? Is that in Sweden?"

"In America. It's a huge chain of high-end stores."

"America again. How odd." Still, a teeny, tiny surge of excitement crept up her spine. Maybe this wasn't going to be such a big humiliating disaster after all.

"And there's a letter from the editor in chief of

Vogue in New York. They'd like to do a spread of you wearing your own clothes for the September issue."

She scrolled down and read it, feeling a surge of heat spread over her face and chest. "How embarrassing. But also wonderful."

"See? Who cares about those dumb paparazzi rags and their pointless websites. You're gaining admirers and buyers where it counts. No one's mentioned numbers yet, but I'd say you have a few million dollars in orders sitting right there in that email account."

"Goodness. I have no idea how to handle that." Once again she was out of her depth. "I don't think Signora Pazzi can sew that fast."

"No." He laughed. "You'll need to hire a factory to produce the items, but remember, they're not delivered until fall so you have time."

She scrolled slowly through the emails. They were mostly from American buyers and one British department store. And at the very bottom was an email from Instituto Marangoni, the fashion school she'd sent an application to.

She decided not to read it. Clearly the Milanese, and maybe all Europeans, hated her style, and she didn't want to lose the glow of discovering that Americans liked it.

"Are you feeling better?" She could hear the amusement in Lorenzo's voice.

"Much better."

"Still think I'm only interested in you for your lake?"

Her joy ebbed somewhat as she remembered the article from earlier. In her frenzy of distress she'd shoved it to the back of her mind. "There was an article in the local paper saying that you applied for planning permission on the lake."

"That was ages ago. And it wasn't for your land. It was for my family's land on the far side of the lake."

"But their land is in Italy, and the permission was applied for in Altaleone." Something didn't add up. Ugly suspicion gnawed at her.

"I don't know what's going on. Maybe they made it up. You know how the press are."

"Yes." She didn't want to get into an argument when he was so far away. And he was probably right. "And I'm glad you told me about the emails. I can't believe I didn't even check. I'm not a very good businesswoman."

"You're a creative genius. You can't do everything."

Beatriz hesitated. Was he implying that he'd be the business side of the operation and she'd do the designing? On the one hand that sounded heavenly. On the other hand, maybe he was just trying to use her and— She stopped her runaway train of thought in its tracks. "I'm a work in progress. And I miss you very much. Good night, Lorenzo."

"Good night, my princess."

After they hung up she scrolled back to the email from Instituto Marangoni. She wondered why they'd sent it to this email and not to her personal one that she'd put on her application. She hadn't wanted Lorenzo to know she'd applied there because—not unlike her dad—he thought fashion school was a foolish waste of her time and she could just hire professionals to do all the heavy lifting. And he hadn't mentioned the email so he clearly thought it beneath her notice.

She opened the message. It was from the director of the institute, not the admissions office. "It has come to my attention that you have contacted our institute. I am taking the liberty of replying personally…" Blah blah blah. Basically, she was being treated differently, as usual, because she was a princess. But instead of admitting her instantly by virtue of her princess card, they'd simply offered her an interview "at her earliest convenience."

She had to laugh. She loved the arrogance of the Milanese fashion world. It was the perfect fit for a proud princess like herself. And dammit, she was going to go on that interview as soon as humanly possible and not tell a single soul about it.

Lorenzo cursed himself for going on this business trip right after her fashion show. What was he thinking? Yes, these meetings had been set up months ago, but his life was different now! Months ago, Beatriz was just a distant and rather supercilious princess who'd blown him off at her brother's coronation.

Now she was the center of his whole world.

He couldn't bear to think of her alone and smarting from the cruelty of the press. Worse yet, she'd warned him from day one that she expected this kind of response. It had never really occurred to him that she might be right.

As wealthy and well-connected as he was, the press could care less what he did or didn't do, and he rarely appeared outside of bland shots in the social pages. He couldn't imagine what it must feel like to live under that harsh and unforgiving spotlight from the day you were born. He'd dismissed her concerns and left her to face their hostility alone.

Pacing back and forth in his hotel room, high over Central Park, he realized he'd been wrong about a lot of things. He should have let Gibran interview him. Why did he care so much about his stupid reputation when Beatriz feelings were at stake? She'd had to make excuses for him to her family after he made them more suspicious than ever. He should have trusted her and gone right to the palace. Maybe he could even have helped their investigation, instead of fighting against it.

An expletive fell from his lips. Sometimes—maybe most of the time—he was too stubborn and arrogant for his own good. When he got his teeth into a good bone—like the lake property—he hung on through thick and thin whether it made sense or not. He was stubborn, like his father, in that way.

But he didn't have to live his life laser focused on goals that didn't make sense anymore. This spring with Beatriz had been the happiest time of his life and already his plans for the future were filled with her— seeing her collection in stores, sailing to the Greek Islands with her this summer, hunting in the mountains next winter...

He let out a sigh so deep that his whole body shuddered. He didn't want her property. He didn't want any damn property near as much as he wanted Beatriz.

He was going to call his assistant tomorrow and have her clear his schedule. Then she was going to prioritize his properties and he'd start selling off his holdings. He'd already made enough money for ten lifetimes and he didn't need to waste his time and energy chasing some invisible brass ring that kept getting further and further away.

His life now was with Beatriz. Yes, there were still some mountains to climb—her brother Darias, for one—but he'd grown up skiing and climbing in the back country and he knew how to tackle the roughest terrain.

And no matter what he had to do, Beatriz was worth it.

20

The next morning Beatriz awoke with a resolve to decline the interview from Instituto Marangoni. The poor reception of her show by the Milanese fashion establishment coupled with Lorenzo's disdain for the idea meant it would only bring criticism and drama into her life.

But her first cup of coffee and the prospect of learning how to cut and stitch and understand the qualities of different fabrics restored her courage. At ten o'clock she called the director of the institute. His assistant put her through immediately and—afraid of losing her nerve again—she scheduled an interview for that afternoon.

Dressed in her usual featureless black uniform, she set out for Milan almost immediately, determined that nothing should stop her. She arrived in Milan with two hours to kill and decided to sit in a café. Since she didn't want to be alone with her thoughts and Nina had to sit there waiting for her anyway, she asked Nina to join her, and they ordered cappuccinos and chatted. It didn't help her nerves that Nina kept wanting to talk about the criminal investigation and the mystery texter, so Beatriz kept changing the subject to something less stress-inducing.

Ten minutes before the interview she walked the short distance to the institute and asked for directions to the director's office. The granite hallways, lined with back-lit floor-to-ceiling fashion images, thrilled her.

Don't get too excited. He might be bringing you in just to torture you. Some people loved the idea of taking royalty down a peg or two. The director's chic assistant ushered her into his office, and she was surprised to find a rather young man, very handsome and serious.

She thrust out her sweating hand and greeted him as calmly as she could manage.

"Princess Beatriz…is that how I should address you?" He lifted a brow.

Anxiety coiled in her gut. "Just Beatriz is fine. I don't want any special treatment. I really want to learn how to work hands on with fabrics and techniques." She didn't want him to think she just wanted to wear the degree like a piece of jewelry.

"I saw your show." He stared at her.

She felt perspiration beading on her brow. "What did you think?"

He smiled. "I'm glad you asked me that instead of launching into a spirited defense of it. I liked it. There was a simplicity that others have criticized, but which I see as the hallmark of a designer who knows that her customer is the jewel in the setting."

Beatriz smiled. "Yes! That's exactly it. I like simple clothing that plays up the woman's figure and beauty, no matter what unique form they take."

"You were surprised by the critical reaction?"

She inhaled and attempted a casual shrug. She didn't want to play the princess card and say they were all haters. "A little. I tried to do some unique things with feathers and use leather that drapes like a fabric."

"Perhaps those ideas were not as original as you thought." He steepled his hands in front of his face. "But I see potential." His brows lowered. "Do you really intend to attend classes all week long like your fellow students? Many of them are here late into the night sewing garments. Surely that would interfere with your official schedule?"

"It would be a challenge, but I'm confident I could rise to it." She decided not to mention the spring line that she'd already started sketching last night to replace the drawings she'd burned. She might have to rent or buy a place in Milan to make juggling everything easier. And why not? Her brothers and sisters had moved all over the world to pursue their dreams.

"Then I'd like to offer you a place at Instituto Marangoni, starting this September."

Beatriz burst into tears.

"That's not quite the reaction I was expecting." He looked amused.

"I'd like to accept." She groped for a handkerchief, trying to stop the hiccupping sobs that racked her body. "I'm so sorry. It's been an emotional week."

"I understand, and congratulations on your first show." When she finally stemmed the waterworks, they had a nice chat about the current Milanese design scene and her orders in the States and he mentioned some current students she should look up and talk to.

Beatriz was floating on air as she took the elevator back down to the first floor and marched out of the institute with a beaming smile on her face.

"I guess it went well," said Nina, as she approached the car.

"I hope you like Milan," said Beatriz, her voice shaky with excitement. "Because it looks like I'm going to be spending a lot of time here."

Now all she had to do was tell Lorenzo. And her family.

Beatriz was exhausted and emotionally spent when she arrived back at the lake house in Altaleone, so she put off sharing her news until the next day. Lorenzo told her two new orders had come in and chided her gently for not checking her email. She refrained from saying that she was too busy dancing on air.

She wanted to tell him about her acceptance to the institute in person because she was a little afraid that if she mentioned it on the phone he might not take it seriously. She asked him to come to the palace the next day so she could share the news with all of them at once.

The next morning she drove to the palace and rode her horse—this time without making the mistake of stopping to read press clippings in her mother's office. She'd finished schooling Gatto and was cooling him out by walking him around the arena when her phone pinged.

Lorenzo's back! She pulled out her phone, a smile already spreading across her mouth. But her feelings of joy shriveled when she saw a menacing message from an unknown number. **I'm watching you, prepare to die.**

Beatriz jumped off her horse, grabbed the reins and led him back into the barn at a trot. This text was a bold threat and cut to the quick. "Nina!" She knew

Nina was nearby since it was her job to keep an eye on her at all times. "Call Gibran."

Nina came running. "What is it?"

"A threat on my phone." Matteo, the groom, appeared out of nowhere, and she handed Gatto to him. "And I never reported the last one I got. I want this traced."

"Let me see." Nina thrust out her hand, and Beatriz put the phone into it. "I'm going to try calling that number."

She pushed buttons while they strode from the stables toward the main palace. For the first time Beatriz felt a cold chill of fear. Her life was going so well—even the sting of the press about the show had subsided—and now this? Wasn't that just how life worked? She'd be on top of the world one minute, lying in a pool of blood the next. And Sandro's shooting was still painfully fresh in her mind. He still sometimes winced from the injury.

Gibran came running, bringing guards who surrounded Beatriz. "Nina sent me the message, and I consider it an imminent threat. All family members are under heavy guard. We're running diagnostics on the number right now, in coordination with the local telecom companies. The text appears to have originated in Zurich, but there are ways to bounce information in order to disguise the location of origin."

Beatriz felt her terror subside a little at the prospect that the texter wasn't even in Altaleone. "I don't know why it scared me so much. It's just a text message."

"In light of the murders, and the attacks on Emma and Sandro, you're all at risk. We're trying to uncover the network of people involved in the suspected conspiracy, but many persons of interest have access to unlimited funds and very good lawyers so we haven't made as much progress as we'd hoped."

The stab at Lorenzo made her look up. Lorenzo was flying back into Zurich today. "You don't still suspect Lorenzo Aldobrando, do you?"

Gibran's stony features didn't reveal a hint of emotion. "Everyone is a suspect until proven otherwise."

Beatriz heard her phone ping in his hand. "Can I see it?"

Gibran glanced at it first before handing it to her. "It's him."

Beatriz looked at the screen, half expecting to see another threat, but this time it was Lorenzo.

Landed and in the car. I'm on my way.

Be careful. Beatriz started shivering. She texted back a thumbs-up sign, not wanting to say more with people watching her. Loose killer aside, her muscles were tense from all the excitement over yesterday's interview and the acceptance, and she was still afraid to even look at the Internet in case she ran across another scathing review of her designs. "Would it be okay if I go take a hot shower?" She didn't want to be sweaty from riding when Lorenzo arrived.

"Of course. Nina will accompany you into your suite."

Beatriz sighed. She truly missed the relative privacy of the premurder days, though maybe it was just because the staff back then were old familiar friends who felt more like family members. All these new security staff made her nerves bristle.

Nina followed Beatriz to her bedroom and locked

the door behind them, then Beatriz went in to run the shower. "I'm afraid you'll have to sit on the chair or something." How awkward having a security guard—even a female one—right in her bedroom.

"Don't worry. I won't let anyone get in here, no matter what." Nina stood just inside the door, her gun drawn."

"I appreciate that." Beatriz hated the sight of guns. The sight of Nina's finger near the trigger gave her a chill.

"I have six years of military training."

"That's great." Beatriz wondered if she should undress in the bedroom like she normally did but decided not to. "I'll be out in a moment."

"Are you sure you don't need me to come in there? There is a window. Someone could climb up."

Beatriz stiffened and attempted a smile but only managed a grimace. "I'll take my chances."

She closed the door behind her, glad Nina hadn't insisted, but also glad she was out there. She'd been so distracted by Lorenzo and her designs and the house that she'd been tuning out the ever-present threat to the royal family. She turned on the shower, undressed and climbed in, glad there was a glass door, not a curtain like the shower scene in *Psycho*.

When she opened the bathroom door, still in her towel, she jumped at the sight of Nina standing in front of the door, gun drawn. "Everything okay?"

"So far."

Nina stepped aside. "Did you get any texts that you haven't mentioned to us?"

Beatriz froze, remembering the previous one that she just hadn't had the energy to deal with. "Just one. Nothing new or different."

"Can I see it?"

Beatriz frowned. It irked her that her phone, filled with intimacies with Lorenzo, could just be commanded by the security staff. Still, she pulled up the thread. **What makes you so sure Lorenzo isn't the murderer?**

She shuddered. She'd totally blocked this one from her mind. It creeped her out that Lorenzo's name was in it and suddenly made her worry about his safety.

She handed it to Nina, who studied it. "This person, whoever they are, always texts you when Lorenzo is on his way."

"Yes, we've already determined that. But I know the texts aren't from Lorenzo."

"How do you know?"

Beatriz frowned. How did Nina know that Lorenzo was on his way when she got this text? "I just know."

"In cases of domestic crime, it's usually the person closest to the victim who is the perpetrator," said Nina softly.

Beatriz stared at her and clutched her towel closer to her chest. "You've spent enough time watching me with Lorenzo to see how much he's done to help me fulfill my goals."

"But why wouldn't he talk to Gibran, even if just to say he's innocent?"

"Because the interview itself puts him under suspicion, as you saw in that article you showed me. I still don't know how that got out." Could have been someone from the courts or the judges office.

No doubt Nina thought her crazy to blindly defend Lorenzo. Isn't that what abused women did for their partners?

"Just know that I'm here to defend you." Nina still held her gun in her hand.

"That's very reassuring," murmured Beatriz, feeling just the opposite. She grabbed some clothes and took them back in the bathroom. Once she was dressed she hurried downstairs as fast as possible, Nina trailing behind her.

It took Lorenzo a long time to drive from the airport, and she texted him several times to make sure he was safe. His car allowed him to listen to texts and respond by voice, so she wasn't putting him in danger. Her nerves jangled with impatience and anxiety. Of course it could be the cheery **I'm watching you, prepare to die** message that she couldn't get out of her head. Obviously that was enough to freak Nina into a heightened state of alert. Darias and Emma arrived, and Darias demanded a fresh briefing from Gibran. Security guards hovered in every corner while she, her mom, Sandro and Serena attempted to distract themselves with wedding ideas and Lucky's antics.

Finally a bustle of staff activity heralded Lorenzo's arrival. Despite his long drive and longer flight, he glowed with health and strength and was a sight for her sore eyes. She gave him the biggest hug she'd ever given anyone.

"I missed you so much. You're not upset about the articles anymore, are you?" He held her in his arms.

"No. I'm over that. They're just jealous haters."

"Did you tell your family about the orders from stores?" Lorenzo lifted a brow and looked at her mom.

"What orders?" Her mom's head cocked.

Beatriz wished she could gag him. She needed to warm them up slowly to this kind of thing so as to avoid a big kerfuffle of how her selling clothing might affect the royal brand. And she didn't want that discussion now. She was bursting to tell him of her acceptance to Instituto Marangoni. "Can I talk to you alone?" she half whispered it, which was silly as there were at least ten people within earshot anyway. Privacy was a pipe dream in a big palace.

"Yes." A tiny wrinkle furrowed his brow. She led him into one of the back sitting rooms that was rarely used since her dad died.

Before she closed the door, he asked. "You got another text?"

She pulled out her phone and showed him. **I'm watching you, prepare to die.**

She sighed. "It's got everyone freaked out, hence the cast of thousands in every room. There's probably someone crouched outside the window ready to defend me with an assault rifle."

"It's a direct threat." He frowned deeply. "But d'you know who I think it is?"

21

"You?" Beatriz lifted a brow. "That's who Nina thinks. It originated in Zurich right when you were there."

"I think it's Nina." Lorenzo fixed those gray eyes on her. "She's always watching you. She follows you everywhere, sees all your movements. And you said the man who shot Sandro was a trusted staff member. Maybe she's part of this conspiracy to disrupt and destroy the royal family."

Beatriz was speechless for a moment. "But...why?"

"Who knows? What do you know about her background?"

"Nothing, but everyone on Gibran's staff is thoroughly vetted. I don't know where she's from, but she's not local. Her accent sounds Scandinavian."

"I've been watching her for a while. She's with you all the time and sometimes I see her looking at you almost possessively. There's something a little off about her."

"Why didn't you say anything?"

"I didn't have any proof, and I didn't want to upset you. But now things have come to a head I'd like to publicly accuse her and see what happens. Is that okay with you?"

Beatriz stomach clenched. "But they trust her. She's been cleared by security. What if they end up throwing *you* in jail?"

"Will you visit me there?" A dark glimmer of mischief shone in his eyes.

"Absolutely." This was no joking matter.

"Then I'll be fine. Trust me." He opened the door and let her walk first back into the living room, past Nina, who was standing nearby in the hallway but not close enough to overhear their conversation. They'd established those space boundaries several weeks earlier—when she was with Lorenzo, Nina needed to stay out of earshot.

"Nina, could you come in?" Lorenzo invited her into the living room. He still had Beatriz's phone in his hand. "As you all know, Beatriz got this message today. *I'm watching you, prepare to die.* She's not dead, and no one has tried to kill her."

"I haven't taken my eyes off her," said Nina proudly.

"I know. You're the one who's watching her, and I believe that you sent this message and the prior threatening text messages."

An angry flush rose up Nina's neck. "Why would I want to do that?"

"Nina has six years of experience in the Norwegian armed forces and no connections whatsoever to Altaleone or this region." Gibran spoke up forcefully. "My staff has been scrutinized to the utmost degree."

Lorenzo kept his stern gaze on Nina. "Then perhaps she wanted to make herself feel more important by inventing a crisis."

Nina swallowed. "It's him. He's the texter. He's an enemy of the family. His family has been trying to get the land she inherited back for centuries. He probably hopes to marry her and then kill her and keep the land."

Beatriz blinked. How did Nina even know about the family feud? Possibly just from listening in on family conversations—especially the blunter ones involving Darias. "That's nonsense. Lorenzo doesn't care about ancient history."

Darias stepped closer. "It's not that ancient, Bea. He did apply for development permission only two years ago."

"For his own land! On the other side of the lake! He only had to ask for permits in Altaleone because his family property directly abuts the crown land. His request had nothing whatsoever to do with my land."

"Except that your land sits right next to his and has better road access, a longer strip of lake shore and more beautiful views of the mountains." Darias lifted his chin, surveying Lorenzo down the length of his aristocratic nose.

"And he wanted to scare her into his arms. To be her hero," blurted Nina.

Lorenzo had the gall to look amused.

"Lorenzo is already my hero." Beatriz was growing exasperated. "And I'm beginning to think that he has a point."

"It could be someone else!" protested Nina. "A murderer in your midst."

"Nina, follow me." Gibran gave a slight nod of his head. They left the room.

"You really think I want your sister for her property?" asked Lorenzo coolly, eyes on Darias.

"Don't you see the vibrant, warm, loving, beautiful woman I see?"

Beatriz's heart swelled.

"Of course I do."

Lorenzo looked right at Darias. "May I speak to you alone?"

"Sure." Darias sounded grudging, but they walked out the same door as Gibran and Nina.

Beatriz looked from her mom to Sandro to Serena. She was bursting to tell someone that she'd been accepted at the *instituto,* but if she told them now, no one would even hear her. "Am I going crazy, or is it everyone else?"

"Both, I suspect," said Sandro with a wink. "But I don't think you need to prepare to die."

She sighed. "I'll try to take comfort in that."

Lorenzo followed Darias into a large study. A large mahogany globe bore a map of the world from a long-gone era. Appropriate since Altaleone sometimes seemed like the land that time forgot.

Adrenaline poured through Lorenzo's veins as he closed the door behind them. Usually so sure of himself, he couldn't tell if he was about to make a fatal mistake. "I'd like to marry your sister."

Darias spun around. "Does she know this?"

"No. I haven't asked yet. Since her father is dead and you are now head of the family, I thought I should ask you."

"Because this is the fifteenth century?"

"Because she's a princess, and I know her first allegiance will always be to her family and to Altaleone."

Darias's stunned and stony expression softened.

"I'm not sure whether to be honored that you chose to ask me first or offended on Beatriz's behalf that you didn't ask her first."

"I have no desire to cause ill will within the family. I'll be blunt. I know you don't like me. From the first you've seen me as an interloper, possibly with some ulterior motive. Just moments ago you accused me of scheming to grab her land. How could I ask her to marry me under these circumstances without clearing the air with you first?"

Darias's brows lowered. "Clearing the air? You think winning my trust will be that easy?"

"No, but I love your sister. I want to make her my wife. I want to be her husband. The press is already starting to talk about us so I don't want to embarrass her by having our relationship turn into a scandal."

"I have no doubt that it already has." Darias stared at him. "What if I said no?"

Lorenzo blinked. He'd anticipated this moment.

"Then I'd attempt to change your mind. As my wedding gift I would give her my family's land on the other side of the lake, along with a contract declaring that all her inherited property remains hers, regardless of Altaleone's patriarchal laws."

Darias's eyes widened. "That property is worth millions."

"Beatriz is worth more to me." A gulp caught in his throat.

"It's an expensive price to pay even for entry into a royal family. In doing this you'd become one of us. Your freedom and independence would be curtailed by duty, and the press will follow your every move."

"I love Beatriz. I love her passion for Altaleone and for all of you."

"And you intend to subordinate your business interests to those of the crown?"

"Absolutely."

"What if I challenge you to a duel?" Darias lifted a brow.

"I'd refuse. I have no desire to kill either a king or my beloved's brother."

"Spoken like a gentleman." A gleam of amusement shone in Darias's eyes. "If you're crazy enough to want to marry my sister, then you have my blessing."

Lorenzo felt a grin spread across his face. "Have you two always had your differences?"

"Since day one." He grinned back. "She's a hard nut to crack and keeps me on my toes, but I wouldn't have it any other way. Now go ask her. Knowing Beatriz she'll probably say no."

Gibran came back into the living room, his bold features like a mask. "Nina has confessed to sending the texts. She sent the first one when she discovered that Beatriz had sneaked off without telling her, wanting to make her take the situation seriously. It worked so well that she sent more to create situations where she felt necessary and important. Only Darias knows that we've been monitoring all texts and calls by palace residents and workers through the local cell company, and she was able to read Beatriz's outgoing texts on the network, in spite of a strict prohibition on reading the family members' private correspondence. Her work for the Norwegian military was in communications so she was able to send texts to Beatriz over the internet using a private browser and a different number every time, and there was no way for us to trace the origin on the cell network. I must apologize for not having uncovered this situation sooner."

"So Beatriz has never been in any real danger?" Lina looked relieved.

"No. And I'm deeply sorry for the distress this has caused all of you."

"I really didn't get that distressed," said Beatriz. "Being royal I'm used to hearing nonsense. What did upset me is how quick everyone was to blame Lorenzo."

Lorenzo appeared in the doorway. "Beatriz, can I speak to you alone?"

"What's with all the secret rendezvous?" asked Sandro. "Serena and I are pregnant. We don't need all this excitement."

"I'll come." Beatriz rose, glad to get out of this room. She followed Lorenzo, who led her down a hallway. "Let's go in here." She led him into a small piano practice room with gold-and-white walls. She knew it was soundproof so no one could overhear them. Finally she could tell him her big news about the instituto and no one would hear the big argument that might follow.

She closed the door and locked it, heart pounding. What if he mocked her plans and told her that taking classes was a waste of time?

I'll break up with him.

Could she? Her existence had changed so completely since Lorenzo came into it that she couldn't imagine life without him. When she wasn't with him she craved the security of his arms around her. Maybe without his support and encouragement she'd retreat back into her shell like a snail?

She screwed up her courage and turned to face

him. "I got an offer yesterday."

He didn't seem to hear her. He had an intense expression on his handsome face and steel shone in his eyes. "Beatriz, will you marry me?"

She froze. Replayed his words in her head to see if she had heard them wrong. No. she heard them right. He really had just asked her to marry him.

Yes. Her body and mind responded with a single chord. She'd barely dared to dream that he'd ever ask her.

But what if he didn't respect her wishes? If he expected her to listen to his advice and follow his guidance as she'd done all along so far.

This time she'd found something that she wanted to do—study the nuts and bolts of fashion—and pursued it on her own. If he didn't want that for her, she'd be giving up a part of herself that she'd only just discovered.

"Yesterday I was offered a place at the Instituto Marangoni."

Lorenzo's eyes widened. He hesitated for a second. "Congratulations."

"I told them I would accept. I know you don't think it makes sense for me to spend the time to go to fashion school, but I want to have the skills and techniques that other designers use to create. I don't want to be the princess who bought her way to the top with the hard-earned skills of others. I want to earn any respect and praise that I get, and be able to shrug off criticism because I know I did things according to my own standards and principles."

"I admire you for that."

"You think I'm crazy."

"I think you're wonderful except that you're

torturing me by not answering my question."

He hadn't really answered hers either. Not that she'd even asked a question. Her decision to go wasn't open to discussion. "Are you okay with me going?"

"Okay with it? I think it's fantastic." He took her hands in his and squeezed them gently. "I promise to support you in everything you desire." He kissed her softly on the lips and her heart melted.

Then he pulled back just enough that he could look her in the eyes. "Woman, are you trying to kill me? I love you so much it hurts. Will you marry me or are you going to break my heart?" The passion in his voice stirred emotion long-buried deep inside her.

"I will marry you." The words drifted out on a whisper. "I love you, too, and I will marry you, Lorenzo."

"Thank God." He swept her into his arms and kissed her so long and hard that they were both breathless when they parted. "I thought Darias would be a hard mountain to climb, but he said yes quicker than you did."

She jerked back, shocked. "You asked my brother?"

"I'm an old-fashioned guy. I'd have asked your father if he were alive." He reached into his pocket and pulled out a tiny sack. "I had this ring made for you." He tipped a ring out into his hand, a big sparkling diamond ringed by tiny black stones. He held it between his thumb and finger. "Do you like it?"

Her full heart ached with joy. "It's stunning." She let him slide it on her finger, where it fit perfectly. "I love the black stones."

"They're black diamonds. I had a local jeweler source them just for you."

"You designed this?"

"I'm not naturally creative, but I had a vision for your ring."

Tears blurred her eyes. "It's perfect." She flung her arms around his neck.

"You're perfect." His words were hot on her neck.

"I'm not even close. And you're pretty pushy and arrogant yourself, but I think we're perfect for each other."

"I couldn't agree more." Their lips met and they kissed each other into passionate and joyous oblivion.

EPILOGUE

"It's probably a good idea to get married before you're pregnant and look like a whale." Serena indicated her midsection. The family sat around the large dining table in the lake house, drinking coffee after a leisurely Sunday lunch.

"I've never seen anyone who looks less like a whale," protested Sandro.

"We're not planning to have a baby right away," said Beatriz.

"We weren't either," said Serena with a wink. "But these little miracles have a way of surprising you."

"We're planning to wait until Beatriz has finished her fashion degree." Lorenzo poured fresh cream in Beatriz's coffee. "She's already very busy getting her collection ready for stores." He beamed proudly.

"I've set up a workshop in Milan to make the really expensive couture garments, and Lorenzo's helped me choose factories in four different countries to accommodate the growing list of orders. I hope it will be a well-oiled machine by the time I start classes in the fall. It feels weird handing the work over to other people."

"It's hard to get used to delegating," said Serena, taking a slice of apricot torte. "I was so used to being a one-woman band that it went against all my instincts to let someone else handle the back-end. I used to spend hours every day just trying to optimize my advertising revenue. Now that I've hired the tedious business part out, all I have to do is record my videos and dictate my blogs, which gives me more time to travel and just enjoy being with Sandro."

"When I first married Darias I thought I'd be sitting around eating bonbons all day, bored out of my mind," said Emma. "But just being royal is a surprising amount of work."

"It's refreshing to hear someone say that." Beatriz laughed. "I think Lorenzo thought I was a slacker when we first met."

"Not true," he protested. "I just realized almost immediately that you had other gifts that you weren't using."

"Speaking of which, I want to design my own wedding dress. And the bridesmaid dresses. I want something sleek and elegant, maybe white satin. Does that sound crazy?"

"It sounds fabulous," said Serena. "My aunt is making me the ultimate frou-frou princess wedding dress so we'll look totally different."

"I want to see yours!" Beatriz had been picking Serena's brain all week for wedding ideas. "Do you have a picture?"

"I don't." She grinned. "I think everyone will have to wait for the wedding day as Aunt Robin is bringing it with her on the plane."

"I'm really enjoying all this wedding planning," said Emma. "Since mine was organized by professionals and done so fast that I didn't even have time to absorb it."

Darias sighed. "It was all Sandro's idea for us to rush into the wedding."

"Hey!" Sandro leaned forward. "Without me you two might never have spoken. Besides, your wedding was beautiful."

"Even though I was trying really hard not to cry the entire time because I was falling hard in love with Darias and I thought he was just marrying me for show."

"My brother can be a little slow on the uptake sometimes," said Beatriz with a wink. "But eventually he comes to his senses."

"True." Darias looked rueful. "I guess I'll be apologizing to Lorenzo for a while. I was kind of a jerk."

"You were a protective brother," said Lorenzo. "Since I have a sister, I can relate."

"I think I was especially ferocious because it's eating away at me that the murders aren't solved yet. I've made Rigo promise to get his butt over here this month."

"He's a lawyer, not a detective," said Beatriz.

"I know, but part of our problem is that our suspects keep wriggling out of being interviewed."

"Like me," said Lorenzo before taking a sip of coffee.

"Exactly." Darias aimed a mock glower in his direction. "If there's no solid evidence, it's hard to question people without violating our constitution. Gibran has sharp ideas but it's hard to follow through on them when your suspects are wealthy bluebloods who keep lawyering up, like the Cross of Blood members. I'm hoping Rigo will find a way to make things happen."

"When's he coming?" asked Sandro.

"Have you seen any winged pigs lately?" asked Beatriz with wink.

"He promised to come for Mom's birthday, but then she ran off to visit Callista in Paris for her big day. Hopefully she won't stay too long."

"I don't know what she's up to there," said Beatriz. "But she seems to be very busy."

"Unusually busy," said Darias. "And she's being infuriatingly mysterious about when she's coming back."

"Good," said Beatriz. "I'm glad she's finally out and about. I felt terrible moving out and leaving her all alone in the palace."

"With only thirty-two staff members to keep her company," muttered Darias.

"You know as well as I do that's not the same thing," said Beatriz. "Sometimes there's nothing lonelier than being surrounded by people who were paid to be there."

"Especially if they're sending you scary text messages predicting your imminent death." Sandro raised a brow.

"Tell me about it! I didn't want to press charges against Nina because she didn't actually do anything worse than waste Gibran's time, but I'm glad she's back in Norway, far away from Altaleone."

"Most people would have been scared out of their wits," said Lorenzo. "Not my Beatriz."

Beatriz shrugged. "Idle threats don't scare me. And critics neither now that we have four million dollars in orders from the American market."

"Seven million," corrected Lorenzo. "But who's counting?"

"Does anyone want to go for a walk around the lake?" asked Beatriz. "We're thinking of turning most of the lake shore into a national park for people from both Altaleone and Italy."

"Maybe we should open it with a ritual joust where Lorenzo and I throw down our lances and ride happily off into the sunset," suggested Darias with a wink.

Lorenzo laughed. "I'm game. It would be a step up from letting you defeat me."

"It was very sporting of you to let me."

"I'd do it again in a heartbeat." He looked at Beatriz, his gray eyes filled with emotion. "It was more than worth it."

THE END

The Royal House of Leone series:
The King's Bought Bride (Darias and Emma)
A Prince for Christmas (Free short story)
The Prince's Secret Baby (Sandro and Serena)
The Princess's Scandalous Affair (Beatriz and Lorenzo)
The Princess and the Player (Carolina and Amadou)
Taming the Royal Beast (Rigo and Bella)

ABOUT THE AUTHOR

Jennifer Lewis is the USA Today Bestselling author of more than thirty novels including the Desert Kings series, the Hearts of the West series and the Billionaires' Secrets series. She loves heat in all its forms including spicy food, steamy temperatures and smoking hot heroes. Her romances have been translated into more than twenty languages, and she especially enjoys seeing them in unfamiliar alphabets where she can't even tell her name from the title. She lives in sunny South Florida and when she isn't writing she's can often be found at the beach. Learn more at www.jenlewis.com.